## Praise for Cynthia Thayer's Novels

# A BRIEF LUNACY

"A real, old-time thriller . . . What a treat it is to read a novel by someone who makes no secret of her interest in a deeper and often darker understanding of the world, a place where, as she knows, a brief lunacy can, and probably will, befall us all."
—*Boston Globe*

"Cynthia Thayer is a writer known for her poetic and affecting prose. It's impressive, then, that she is able to cross over into the literary thriller genre with such ease and agility. . . . Discomfiting yet gripping in so many ways."
—*Pages*

"Startling, revelatory." —*Kirkus Reviews*

"A well-spun tale, believable and horrifying . . . a suspenseful and tight story that is sure to leave anyone a little leery of opening the door to strangers in need."
—*Times Daily*, (Florence, AL)

"Cynthia Thayer is a novelist I have admired from the publication of her first novel. *A Brief Lunacy* is an impressive leap for her. Though very much connected to her previous work in sensibility, this is a contemplative thriller with all the page-turning suspense of *The Desperate Hours* as the past bubbles up into the present."
—Katharine Weber, author of *The Little Women*

*For Thelma, with best Wishes*

# A Brief
# Lunacy

❖

A NOVEL BY

CYNTHIA THAYER

*Cynthia Thayer*
8/23/14

DELTA TRADE PAPERBACKS

A BRIEF LUNACY
A Delta Book published by arrangement with
Algonquin Books of Chapel Hill

PUBLISHING HISTORY
Algonquin Books of Chapel Hill Hardcover edition published March 2005
Delta Trade Paperback edition / March 2006

Published by
Bantam Dell
A Division of Random House, Inc.
New York, New York

Library of Congress Catalog Card number: 2004059783

ISBN-13: 978-0-385-33964-3
ISBN-10: 0-385-33964-X

Printed in the United States of America
Published simultaneously in Canada

www.bantamdell.com

BVG    10  9  8  7  6  5  4  3  2  1

To my children,

and
to the memory of the thousands of Roma,
taken in the night from the Gypsy camp
at Auschwitz-Birkenau
to the gas chambers
on August 2, 1944

## ACKNOWLEDGMENTS

Many thanks, first and foremost, to members of my stellar writing group: Annaliese Jakimides, Christopher Barstow, Paul Markosian, Kristin Britain, David Fickett, Thelma White, and Bettina Dudley, who listened, agreed, disagreed, suggested, and supported, and without whom this book would not exist.

To my supportive husband, Bill, first reader after my writing group and staunch advocate of "a room of my own."

To my friend Linda Kimmelman, for help in interpretation of Biblical passages.

To my fabulous agent, Sandy Choron, for her faith in my work and her enduring friendship.

To my editor, Andra Olenik, for her astute editing suggestions, and her ability to hear what's exactly right.

# A BRIEF LUNACY

# 1

## JESSIE

TWO YOUNG GULLS prance on the boulder outside my kitchen window, tossing a dead fish back and forth. The others stand, one-legged, facing the spot on the far shore where the sun will emerge. Sometimes I imagine that it won't rise at all and the light will remain dim throughout the whole day. Tranquil October mornings are my best time for thought.

Before the telephone rings or Carl fills the kettle with water, I sit at the painted yellow table, without tea, without the clatter of breakfast dishes, without a living soul to speak to. Sometimes I write in a handmade book filled with pale green paper given to me by Sylvie last Christmas. I keep the sweet card she sent tucked in toward the back of the book. But I am tired. I don't write anything. The book lies flat open on the place mat.

Today I just sit and look at my hands. When I touch the

skin on the back of my hand between the long bones, the spot feels puffy; the skin, brittle. If I saw those hands in a magazine photograph, I would say they were the hands of an old woman, and I'd be right. It surprises me, that's all.

"Carl." I know he's awake, so I don't raise my voice. Just call loudly enough to let him know I'm starting the omelet. The first egg yolk breaks when I crack its shell against the bowl rim. The next two are perfect. I shake a little extra pepper and dried thyme into the bowl before I beat the eggs.

He comes clattering up behind me with the teakettle. I keep grating the cheese. He runs too much water into the kettle every morning and it takes forever to boil. After he lights the gas, he stands behind me and presses his mouth to the back of my neck and hums. Every day.

"Good morning, my pet," he says.

"Carl? Why do the gulls face the rising sun?"

"Because they know it's going to be a day full of fish."

"Tomato in your omelet?"

"Not today. I've got a canker from all the tomatoes. How about some of the smoked salmon from last night?"

That's what I love about him. He doesn't say, *Sure, tomato would be fine.* And he gets the smoked salmon himself from the refrigerator, unwraps it, and places it on the cutting board in front of me. I slice it into tiny pieces while the omelet sizzles in the frying pan and the teakettle hums to boiling. We're a team, Carl and I.

"What are you doing today?" I ask him.

"Nothing," he says. "Nothing planned."

Funny. For years there was no question of what was to be

done on any given day. Monday: go to work. Tuesday: go to work. Saturday: rake the yard, clean the garage, play tennis if there was time. I taught history to high school seniors. Carl was a surgeon who replaced knees and hips with metal and plastic. We worked hard. Now we don't.

Even when I was a child, days were mapped out for my brother and me. My dad was a teacher at Wheaton College and my mother died delivering us. Harry and I were the only children, but they say twins are enormously difficult to raise. It was true. After Harry's accident, I wasn't very well behaved and Harry needed constant attention until his hip healed. In the summer we took trips to educational places like Gettysburg and the Grand Canyon. During the school year, I took ballet and piano and figure skating. Harry took drawing and sculpture. I should have taken the art lessons, I suppose, because that's what I love to do. But Harry took them because he couldn't dance or skate or run.

Dad never married again. He had friends. A few serious women friends. But I think he felt he had to compensate for our having no mother. In a way, Harry and I were mothers to each other. What a strange thought.

"About time to go see Sylvie, *n'est-ce pas?*"

"Next week," I say. "The last time, well, it wasn't easy."

"She expects us. We haven't been for a couple of months."

"Not now, Carl. Some other time."

Last Thanksgiving was a nightmare. The children were all here. Sam. Charlie and his wife. My brother, Harry, and his wife. Sylvie. It took both Carl and Charlie to hold her, to keep her from burning the place down.

I set the table with plates and cloth napkins and my mother's china teacups. "Let's paint in the woods. Just take the easels down the path and paint some of the mushrooms before they rot. There's a fox skull down by the old pine. I'd like to do something with that."

We sit on opposite ends of the long, thin table, the smoked salmon and cheese omelet on a platter between us, the teapot steaming. He places his glasses on the windowsill before he helps himself. Some days, like today, he looks too large to fit in a chair. People used to remark that he was too big to be a surgeon, that his hands were more suited to moving hay bales. Carl laughed at them and told them to think about Oscar Peterson and his sausage-sized fingers playing piano better than anyone else in the world.

"Still water today," he says. "Not a ripple."

"No. Not a ripple."

"Quite a chunk of fish the young ones have."

"Look. That adult just brought another. Look. There on the rock."

The Earl Grey tea smells smoky, like old cigars and Harris Tweed, like professors at grad school. I pour mine first, as Father always did, because the first pouring is the weakest.

Carl's skin is old, too. I touch the back of his hands.

"Jessie? What's up?"

"Nothing. Just touching you," I say.

"Sure, we can go to the woods. Oils or water?"

"Watercolor today. I prefer watercolor."

"The tree?"

"Yes. Of course. The tree."

Last year we both took a drawing class at the library with an artist who lives in New York in the winter and comes here for the summer. Funny, I can't remember his name, but he's famous. We drew paper bags for eight weeks. At the time, I thought that was excessive, but we learned patience and how to see something as it truly is. We crumpled bags. We smoothed them out. We stacked them one on the other, hid them behind each other, pushed one inside another. The teacher kept saying to draw what was really there, not what we thought should be there. When we learn that, we can draw what's in our mind. I'm still stuck at barely drawing what is really there, but I think Carl has graduated to drawing what he imagines there. It will come, Carl says.

Breakfast takes a long time. We sip tea and nibble at our eggs. He toasts a stale bagel. I pour us both more Earl Grey as the gulls continue to watch the sunrise and make plans for their day. Another young gull has joined the fray, vying for fish. Do birds really wonder what they will do in the afternoon? Decide if they will fly over to Schoodic Rock or to Little Sheep? Or does the chief gull just take off and the others follow?

While Carl cleans up the breakfast dishes, I open the top drawer in the red chest and sort through the paints. Someday soon I'm going to organize this blasted drawer and throw away the dried-up tubes and empty jars and stiff brushes. Because it's October, I choose browns and reds and yellows with white to make colors like coffee and brick and canary.

Carl sings while he washes the dishes. Usually he sings

old tunes like "Blue Moon" and "Let Me Call You Sweetheart," a little off key, but today he sings in French. He spent his early childhood in France. Now he changes to a children's song in a small voice, like a child's, words that I can't understand. How do I know it's a children's song? It just is. Such a sweet thing, to sing a children's song. You can tell even if you don't know the words. Kind of mournful and sung in a peculiar key, a different language. Maybe Spanish. Where would he have learned Spanish? I don't think I've heard it before. He speaks German, too, and a bit of Polish because of the time he spent there during the war, but he hardly ever uses it. When he's upset about something, he swears in Polish.

The canvas bag has everything we need. We each have a portable easel that Charlie gave us for Christmas. I tell the children that we don't need anything, because they usually get us something useless, but we do use the easels. One year Sam gave us a very expensive book about Siberia. We bring it out and put it on the coffee table when he comes to visit. Another coffee-table book.

Carl carries the canvas bag with the paints and paper and easels, not because I'm not strong enough, but because he's taller and the bag doesn't bump along the tops of the stumps and stones as we walk.

"What's the song about? The one you were singing?"

"Oh, I don't remember. Something about a little bird."

"Your mother sang it to you?"

"Yes. My mother."

"French?"

"Yes. French."

But I'm not sure it's French. I studied French for years and I didn't recognize even one word. No, I think it's another language entirely. But I don't ask again. Carl is kind of exotic. There are things about him that I don't know. I love to imagine all kinds of possibilities, like that he was the prince of some foreign land or was kidnapped by the Russians and held against his will. What I do know is that he had a hard time of it during the war.

Wet leaves cover the outcropping granite and I'm afraid I'll fall. I wrap my fingers around the edge of his jacket, which of course is ridiculous because if I slip I will pull him down with me, but it makes me feel safe.

"Should we get another dog? We don't have to get a puppy."

"It's too soon. Maybe in the spring," he says.

Reba's only been dead a month. How long do you wait before it's proper to get another dog? Who decides these things? She was a big golden retriever who wouldn't retrieve and hated the water. Carl said some other breed got in with the mother for a quickie and Reba's father wasn't really a golden at all but some poodle or Irish wolfhound. We both cried out loud when we found her dead the morning of September fourth under the kitchen table. Carl said some expletive in Polish when he pressed his palm against Reba's cold forehead. I wish I spoke another language. When I got my Master's degree I had to read French, but that's not like speaking it.

"There won't be many more days we can paint outside,"

he says. "We'll have to paint the ocean from the kitchen table."

"Here we are," I say, as if he wasn't aware that we had arrived at the old pine tree. "It's still there. Do you think it will fall?"

"Fall?"

"The tree. The pine tree. Sylvie's tree."

"Jess, my love, that tree's been there for years."

"But the lower limb. It's got a crack in it."

"Jess, all things fall over and die sometime. That old tree will. But not today."

This place is damp. It reminds me of the swamp where Harry and I used to hide from the bad guys. Once, our father had to gather the neighborhood for a search. They found us soaking wet and covered with scratches. There weren't really any bad guys and it's not really a swamp here, but the smell is the same. Damp leaves. Rotting ferns. Seaweed from the nearby shore. A place where the living turn into the dead to feed the living.

"There's mushrooms all over the place," Carl says.

"I'm going to get the fox skull," I say. "It'll only take a minute."

The only sound I hear behind me is Carl setting up the easels. I've forgotten exactly where I left the skull, but I follow the narrow game trail through the alders, watching on the left for a stump with bones on top. I gather bones of dead animals. Isn't that crazy? The fox skull is the most exciting. Why? I don't know. Perhaps because I can hold it easily in my hand and imagine where the tongue was and what the teeth chewed on. I load the skull, plus the fragments of legs and ribs and wings I've gathered, into the front of my jacket. Near the stump are some pinecones and clumps of chartreuse moss that I pile onto the bones until there's no more room.

It reminds me of when I was pregnant with Sylvie and thought I couldn't get any bigger without bursting, and I balanced a mug on my belly at breakfast. Carl thought it was a riot but always checked to make sure the tea wasn't hot enough to burn me. I wanted to name her after his mother, Chantal, but he didn't want to. He said he had no family. Carl chose *Sylvie.* He'd always liked the name, he'd said. I wonder how it would have been with her if we'd named her Chantal. *Sylvie,* like *sylvan,* the woods, the moss, natural like the deer and the coyote. Sylvie was like the woods when she was small. She picked up sticks and leaves and small bones and tucked them into her pockets. Her whole village was made from debris she found in the woods and on the shore. Whatever happened to it?

The alders blur ahead of me and I'm not sure of my way. My load shifts and some of the cones spill onto the ground. Ahead through the trees I hear Carl rustling around getting ready for the morning. I hear him pouring tea from the thermos. Has it come to this? Nothing important to do? Painting bones and moss and mushrooms on big sheets of bleached paper that will be thrown out when we die by children who thought we were just keeping busy?

"Carl, I've got a load here."

"My darling, let me help."

Everything is set up: the portable stools that we bought at the flea market and the easels from Charlie and the canvas bag that we spread out and cover with tubes of paint organized by color.

"Be careful, my pet, not to kick the water over."

I tiptoe around the paints and canvas to my spot. I thought I might paint the tree today but it's really Carl's subject. The closest branch hangs lower than usual because of the break. The last storm, I think. It won't last long. I wonder if we should get some new wire and tie it up. Sylvie will be distraught if the limb breaks. But I say nothing. Perhaps after we are finished painting. Or perhaps tomorrow. Or in the spring.

I set up my still life beside a rotting bolete, lean the cracked wing bone against the black side of the mushroom, tear off a small section of the chartreuse moss, place it in front of the bone.

"Too much balance," he says.

"What do you mean?"

"Here."

He pulls the piece of moss away from the bone and places it closer to the mushroom, and it is better, unbalanced, uneasy, more exciting. I don't think I'm very exciting. I sit down on the stool and dip my brush into the water and start to paint.

# 2

## JESSIE

JUST AS I BEGIN my second still life, I sense something new in the woods, a sound or a presence or perhaps a change of weather. Carl glances my way to see why I've stopped painting. "It's nothing," I tell him. "Just thinking about the mushroom." I move the stool so that I can view my still life from another direction and tear off the sheet to expose a blank one.

"I think it's too difficult to have Sylvie home for Thanksgiving, don't you?"

"Then let's go down the day before and visit," he says. "I'll bring her a painting of the pine tree. Remember how she loved to climb way up? And the tree house that we built? There. Look. A board's still hanging from that high branch."

I don't respond about the tree. And what's the point in giving her the painting? "Sam's bringing his new girlfriend. Did I tell you?"

"Yes, you did. A medical student, isn't she?" He holds up a dark green painting. "How do you like this one?"

"Very nice. They won't be here until early Thanksgiving morning. Renting a car in Boston and spending the night on the road. That will give us time to get back from seeing Sylvie. Do you think it's wrong to not want her here? It will just be too much with the new girlfriend and everything else."

"What's that you said?"

"Just mumbling to myself."

I'm scared to have her home. Last Thanksgiving, Sylvie came home the week before because she wanted to help with dinner. We picked up a free-range turkey from a farm down the road, and the day before Thanksgiving, Sylvie and I baked pies and made stuffing. We made pecan pie and deep-dish cranberry pie and a pumpkin pie with Frangelico and a ginger crust. Sylvie chopped nuts and baked the pumpkin. She made a papier-mâché turkey for the centerpiece.

"Mom," she said. "This is fun. I want to come home. You know, live at home. With you and Pop. Wouldn't that be great?"

Had I ever been so hopeful as I was that day? I'm not sure. I truly believed it would, in fact, be great. But could I have really been thinking it would last? That we would make meals together and knit by the fire in the evenings? Sometimes mothers hope against hope for their children.

On Thanksgiving morning, Charlie arrived with Madeline, his wife of seven years, and her mother, Mrs. Lachaby, as she insisted on being called, and Harry and his wife. Well, after all, the mother's husband had just died and she had nowhere to go. Sylvie was fine. She and Carl went for a walk along the shore before dinner. They were stunning together, hand in hand, father and daughter. It was almost a dance, the two together, she light as silkweed, he steady as stone. I watched them until they disappeared behind the granite boulders.

When they came back I could see she was edgy. Charlie was basting the bird when it happened. It began as swearing. Just pacing and light swearing about holidays and turkeys and the world in general. I tried to tell Mrs. Lachaby to leave it alone, just ignore it, and I went on chatting about Maine in November and how stark the landscape was. But she didn't get it.

"Do you allow her to behave in that manner?"

"She's an adult," I said. "I can't allow or disallow."

"Well, I think it's deplorable conduct. Madeline, were you aware of Sylvie's behavior? Has this happened before?"

"Mother, let it be. Give her some space."

"Does this kind of thing run in families? Sylvie. Can't you calm yourself, young lady?"

"Well, fuck you, Miss Pig," Sylvie said. "Mommy? Tell her. Tell her to leave me alone."

"Sylvie, darling," Harry said, "let's you and your old uncle Harry go for a walk."

"Please, Mrs. Lachaby, have some patience. She is ill."

"Oh, ill, is it?" Sylvie said. "Is that what you call it? I'll show you ill." I'm glad she chose the cheesecake, because it was soft and easy to clean up. And I'm glad she threw it at me and not at the mother of our daughter-in-law. After that, Sylvie said she'd take a bath and calm down. She'd be fine after her bath.

Sylvie made a little bonfire in the bathroom with dry pine needles from her pocket and a bunch of drawing pencils from the art drawer. She wanted to keep the people who lived in the bathtub warm. She exploded when we said there were no people living in the bathtub. Carl and Harry brought her to the hospital and made it back in time for dinner. But it was all very distressing. The holidays were never very good times with Sylvie. Something about the time of year.

We paint for the whole morning, and for the entire time, I hear things in the woods. Not squirrels or birds, either. Once, I think of calling out, *Who's there? Is anyone out there?* but Carl's right beside me painting the pine tree over and over again. It's funny. He's the one who paints the tree but I'm the one who loves it. By noontime we each have a stack of watercolors. His are all of the pine tree. Mine are of bones and mosses and cracks in the pine bark. Carl says we could have a two-person show at the library next summer. Yes. We could.

On the way back to the house for lunch, I walk behind him because he's bigger and breaks the way through the bushes. And besides, I love to watch his back as he tromps through the woods. I wouldn't ever tell anyone that I find my husband sexy at our age. But that's the truth of it.

I try to picture him as a young boy, running away fast as

he can on sickly legs, his mother yelling, *"Vite, vite!"* for him to run faster, faster, and his father blocking the bullets behind him. Did he keep running when he heard the shots? When he heard the rest of his family drop to the ground? When he noticed that his mother's voice no longer urged him on? He never told me the details. I only know that little bit because I pried too hard once when we'd had too much champagne. And I've seen the fish on his arm and the scars on his back. There's no mistaking those things. Sometimes I'm satisfied not knowing very much because it's clear it's a life he's set aside, but sometimes I want to prod and snoop. But where do I do that? I don't think he has anything from that time except for the violin.

It was during the war. When I think of it all, I cry. I can't help it. And right now I want to yell at him in English to run fast, but I know I can't do that. There's no reason to worry except for the feeling I have that there's something in our woods that doesn't belong here.

As we approach the house, I half expect Reba to dash off the porch to greet us. It's like when I quit smoking. Every time the phone rang, I'd reach for a cigarette, although there weren't any and I wouldn't have smoked one anyway. Sometimes even today that happens to me, after twenty-two years of not smoking. Reba's only been gone for a month. Do you suppose I'll be watching for her twenty-two years from now?

"What's that, Jessie?"

"I'm just laughing at myself," I say.

"Shall I slow down?"

"Why would you do that?"

"I don't know."

"Carl? Do you hear something?"

"Crows. Gulls. Your footsteps. That's the best sound. Your footsteps." He turns around. "My Jess. What do you hear?"

"I thought I heard someone. A person. A dog. It's nothing."

He kisses my forehead before he turns back on the trail toward the house, which seems oddly alone on the small hill overlooking the bay. I can see from here that the gulls have gone off for the day, probably to Schoodic Rock or down to the sardine factory to scrounge more fish.

We clatter and bang our way into the house, dragging easels and finished canvases and paints up the back stairs and into the kitchen.

The answering machine blinks by the kitchen phone. Three messages. The first is the library reminding me about the overdue mystery. I delete it. The second is Sylvie.

"Mommy? Are you there? I've left the fucking place. Everyone there's a nutcase."

"What?" Carl says.

"I'm on the way to the Midwest. Isn't that a riot? Going to North Dakota," she says. Her voice is sweet, lyrical, like when she was a child. "I have money and I know how to get more. I can dance."

"Yes, my darling," I say to the machine. "You can dance."

"Don't, Jess. She can't help it. There's nothing we can do."

"And guess what?" There's a long pause, as if she expects us to pick up the phone. "There's a guy here in the loony bin who loves me. How about that?"

"Oh, Sylvie, I love you," I say.

"Loves me loves me loves me," she sings. The tune is familiar but I can't place it. "Yes, he loves me, yeah, yeah, yeah." It's a Beatles tune.

"Sylvie, where are you?" Do I expect her to answer?

" 'Bye, Mommy. Dad. He's leaving, too."

"Who, dear?"

Carl presses the button for the next message. Is Sylvie finished? He hardly gives her time to say good-bye.

"Mrs. Jensen? This is Rita at Douglas House. I'm sorry to worry you but please call as soon as possible. Hello? Are you there?"

There are more "hello"s before Rita from Douglas House finally hangs up.

"What? Sorry to worry us? Worry that Sylvie left? Sorry she is insane? Sorry she's not Sylvie, sylvan of the woods, tree climber?"

"Jess. Compose yourself. We'll find her. She never goes where she says she's going. You know that. She won't go to North Dakota."

"Carl. She's in the woods."

"No. Jess, why would she be in the woods? How would she get here? She isn't in the woods."

"Call the place. You call. You're better at these things."

We both sit down, as if an outward appearance of calm will translate through the phone lines to the bureaucracy. I pull the sock out of my knitting bag, thankful that I'm not at the turning-the-heel place, thankful that I have several inches to go on the leg before I need to think. Carl leans back in his chair, pen and paper in his lap. Only my knitting needles move; their clicking is the only sound.

"Rita, please," he says when someone answers. "Carl Jensen here."

They know nothing at all. Isn't that why they get paid? To know what happens to their patients? Carl waves me away when I try to ask the questions, Where is she? Why did she leave? Does she have her medication? When was she last seen? He listens intently, writes on the pad little notes in doctor writing that no one else can read. When I peer over to try, he shifts his weight so that I can see, but it's just lines, dots, dashes. I recognize nothing about where or when or why.

I drop a stitch. My fingertips feel numb on the yarn and I have to use a crochet hook to pick up the loop before I continue going around and around on the three needles. The noise of the clicking makes me a bit crazy myself but I'm afraid to sit with nothing. I've never been one to be idle, to clasp my hands in my lap.

"Please let us know if you hear anything," he says into the telephone.

"Of course they'll let us know," I say after he hangs up. "What a stupid thing to say."

His face flushes as if I'd slapped him. "They're looking in all the usual places," he says.

"I'm sorry, Carl. I didn't mean to say that."

"I know, my pet. Of course you didn't."

"Now what do we do?"

"You could finish the sock," he says.

# 3

# J E S S I E

THE WAIT IS INTERMINABLE and the socks are finished. Useless balls of yarn, too small for anything but trim or accent, roll around at the bottom of the basket. Then I remember the paper bag in the car with the Donegal tweed yarn that I bought to make Sam a sweater, and some skeins of primary colors for socks. I'm afraid to leave the phone to get the yarn and I hesitate to ask Carl to do it for me because it sounds like such a frivolous errand.

"Shall I heat the chowder?" he asks.

"No," I say. "I'll do it." Thank God he asked about the chowder, because the inordinate hush is disconcerting. On the way to the kitchen I lift the receiver, just to make sure it wasn't replaced off kilter. That happens sometimes.

The kitchen is as we left it this morning, which seems strange to me because now life has changed. Wouldn't you think the kitchen would appear darker or lighter or disturbed in some way? I know this has happened with Sylvie before but that doesn't make it any easier. The table creaks when I lift one end and swing it toward me, away from the wall, just to shift the focus when we sit to have lunch. A change of scenery. Look at things from a new angle. You have to do that sometimes.

Just last night we sat here sipping too-hot fish chowder and eating fresh biscuits, chattering about Sylvie, saying we hadn't heard from her in a while and how that seemed like a good sign. The chowder is thicker today as it falls from the bowl into the saucepan, chunks of potato and haddock plopping into the bottom, splashing milk onto my sweater. Some splatters the lenses of my glasses and I can't see the chowder in the pot.

Carl is right. We always find her. She gets picked up on the street or she calls us from a stranger's house a few minutes away from Douglas House. They can't really keep her locked up, because she isn't a danger, they say. Just crazy. Just out of touch with reality.

When I put the pot of chowder on the top of the gas stove and turn the heat on very low, I take off my glasses and sit at the table to wait. My fingers close around my glasses tight enough to break them but I don't hear any cracks or snaps except in my own brain. Why don't they break? I pound the glasses down on the table and a lens falls out in my hand. Now they're broken. That's reality, *n'est-ce pas?* as Carl would say.

"You all right over there?"

"Right as rain," I say. "Waiting for the chowder."

When I was in labor with Sylvie, I wanted chowder and all the hospital had was cheese sandwiches. The doctor said not to eat anything because it would make me sick. Sylvie was big. I remember that. They knocked me out with ether and wouldn't let Carl in the delivery room even though he was a doctor. While I lay there on the table, my arms tied to keep them out of the way, legs tied to keep them open, invaded with forceps and strangers' fingers, Carl went out to the Norfolk Restaurant and bought a triple takeout of fish chowder.

I think my own mother bled to death. Because we were too big. Why couldn't they stop the bleeding? I think my father was with her. Were we there or did they take us away? As a child I imagined my mother cradling us, one in each arm, as my father wiped her cheeks with a damp towel and she whispered that she loved us with her last dying breath. I've gotten over that but I still picture her touching us, placing her fingers in our small fists. I've never asked my father if she saw us. I don't want to know that she didn't.

Sylvie was pretty: dark like Carl, and elfin, her face framed with black hair, which the nurses had to trim because they were afraid it would hurt her eyes. Her fingers waved in the air like dancing ferns. And I couldn't even eat the chowder Carl brought. He ate it all himself except for one spoonful that he fed to me. I couldn't seem to eat anything but toast.

Carl doesn't ask why the table is askew or why my glasses have a lens missing. Sometimes I wonder if he notices things like that or whether he just doesn't mention them because he's grown accustomed to my odd habits. We chat about Sam and whether the girlfriend can pay for her own medical school and about Charlie's new appointment as partner at McGinty, Trainor, and Hoyt. Carl gets up once to check the receiver. We don't speak of the telephone until we finish eating.

"I'm going to go outside," I say. "Will you listen for the phone?"

"Where are you going? She's not out there. How would she get here?" He slurps his soup. Carl is a good man but he slurps his soup.

"Just a walk. Breath of air, and I need to get my yarn from the car. Call me if you hear anything. I'll be back soon."

I half-wittedly hold the door behind me for the dead dog and kick dry leaves from the landing, where they pirouette to the ground. The sun has dried the night dew from the forest. Small noises surround me as I make my way through shriveled ferns toward the pine tree. I stop here and there to listen to rustlings made by squirrels and birds and perhaps mice. Nothing sounds big like a human being walking. Carl is right. She couldn't come all the way here by herself.

My still life has collapsed. I gather dry leaves into a pile at the base of the tree and lower myself onto them. I'll just sit quietly and listen to what comes. A woodpecker hammers in the next tree. I hiss at it to shut up. If there were someone in the woods, I wouldn't hear them over that racket. I shift my weight, unfold my legs, which have fallen asleep, and stretch them out in front of me. My foot kicks the old broken wing bone.

"Sylvie? Are you out here?"

The woodpecker racket ceases. The small rustles disappear. There is nothing. I'm not sure what I expect.

"Look at me, Mommy." It's a little girl's voice I hear in my head, not my grown daughter who is crazy, hiding in the woods. "Look how high I am." And I looked and said, "Oh, my. You certainly are a climber." And afterward we walked through the woods, her small hand tucked in mine, while she gathered her "collection," as she called it, a tote bag heavy with stones and chipmunk tails and clods of moss. In those days, we lived here only for a few weeks in the summer in a cabin we built ourselves. Sylvie set up a whole village of people and houses made from sticks and bones and feathers in the middle of the living room floor. Did we know something then? Harry said it was strange for a child to set up a disparate world like that. Sam and Charlie knew to stay away from her village, and each year it grew larger and more complicated until the year she was twelve. One day we came back from town and everything was gone. The only sign was a moldy spot in the center of the braided rug. She never spoke of it. When I asked where her village was, she said she was grown up and had no need for such things. Should I have talked to her about that? I guess we should have.

The next year, Sylvie burned the place down.

Then I hear it again. A footstep, perhaps. The snap of a stick. A breath that is not mine.

"Hello? Sylvie? It's Mommy."

I struggle to my feet because my legs are all pins and needles from sitting so long. No one answers. I look up but I can't see anything. My glasses. "Come down, darling." If I had my glasses I could see better. A pinecone drops from the tree and sticks to my sweater. Is that the noise? Pinecones dropping?

All the way back to the house I listen for her, but I know she isn't there. She would appear if she saw me. She'd laugh and throw her head back, and for a moment I'd think she was little Sylvie of the woods with her tote full of doll parts. But after the laugh would come anger and swearing and then perhaps a lost look and a tilt of her head. "Mommy?" And she'd run to me and kiss my eyelids. Once, after the kiss she bit me. Not hard. But Carl noticed the marks.

Carl sits at the end of the kitchen table, receiver to his ear, twirling my broken glasses around and around through the empty lens hole. He's talking to Charlie at the office, asking if he's heard anything. Now, why would Sylvie contact Charlie?

"Will we see you on Thanksgiving?" he says. "Well then, bye, Son. We'll keep in touch."

"Why are you using the phone? What if she calls?" I sit down in my chair. "What if she's trying to reach us?"

"Here, Jess. Have some tea." He pours steaming tea into my breakfast cup. "I just thought they might have heard something. Charlie's her brother, after all."

"Should we go to Bangor? Should we go searching?"

"Where? Where would we start?"

"Anywhere. The police. Churches. Hospitals."

"They're looking for her. Did you get your yarn? You could start another sock."

"Did Rita call again?"

"No."

"But you've been on the phone."

"How about Scrabble? It'd pass the time."

"Would you drive up the lane to the highway? Just see if she's trying to come to us. It's a long walk down here. What if she fell?"

"I do hear something now," he says.

"Who would be knocking? Who?" There has been no car sound. And we're over a mile from the road.

# 4

## J E S S I E

WHILE MY FINGERS are still wrapped around the doorknob, the knock happens again. Sometimes she knocks. Isn't that odd that a child would knock at her own home? Which Sylvie will it be, elf of the woodlands or queen of the venomous mouth? Although I know there is no God, I pray for the sweet creature who kisses me too hard.

Hans stands just outside the door on the stoop, his ridiculous walking stick held upright, his bare knees bowed out. Who would wear shorts this late in the season?

"Come in, Hans," I say. Carl can't stand him. "Would you like coffee?"

"I'm off caffeine," he says. "I'll take hot water. Everything all right here?"

He strides into the house toward Carl, tapping the infernal stick on our shiny floor with every step. He makes an exaggerated swerve around the piled-up tubes and paintings left in a heap by the cabinet. Why did I invite him in? I don't know. Why can't I say, *It isn't a good time, dear friend*? But he isn't even a dear friend. He stands at the table, waiting to be invited to sit down with Carl. Carl gazes out toward the absent gulls, picks up yesterday's newspaper, reads the back page again. When I catch his eye he nods my way, pushes out a chair for Hans, and resumes reading. Carl is very rude sometimes but I love him. Why? Because he loves me and he's kind to most people.

"Well now," I say. "How is Marte?"

"She was going to come walking but she fell yesterday and her knee is swollen."

"Oh, that's too bad."

"She goes to Boston tomorrow. Visit with the kids."

Carl says nothing at all. One of the gulls lands on a nearby rock and stares through the window.

"She says to come for cocktails at six."

"Not today," I say. "We have some family business going on."

"More problems with the daughter?"

"Not *the* daughter." Carl speaks as if he is lecturing to a class of idiots. "*Our* daughter, and now isn't a good time to chat. And her name is Sylvie."

"I know that," he says.

"Would you like a biscuit?" I ask.

"Thank you, yes," Hans says.

"I'm not sure you have time for a biscuit," Carl says.

"Oh, Carl. Don't be rude."

"Sorry about invading," Hans says. "I'll tell Marte you were asking for her. Another time."

I see him to the door. I wish Carl hadn't told him about Sylvie. I would have left it at *Just family business*. It's really no one else's concern. Hans paid no attention to Sylvie when she was young, but he stopped in a few summers ago when Sylvie was visiting and they took a liking to each other.

I stand in the open doorway waving as Hans walks along the path that leads past the old pine tree and continues toward his house, which is several miles down the shore. He has nothing else to do but walk. And what if Sylvie is there, by the tree? Perhaps it was Hans that I heard in the woods.

"Why did you tell him? About Sylvie?"

"I didn't say a word about her."

"It's not his business."

"All I said was her name. I said not to call her 'the daughter.'"

"Next time, please—"

The telephone rings. Carl answers it. I can tell it's Rita again and that she knows nothing. Now I sit at the table, drum my fingers on the surface, listen to Carl on the telephone. He asks questions and listens politely. Outside, the shadows of the trees lengthen as dusk settles all around. Where is she? When the children were young I sometimes thought about our old age, when they would have their own families and careers, and imagined Carl and I sitting by our fire, sipping our wine, thinking about what a wonderful family we raised together. Now we are old and we sit and worry about our firstborn, who has no family of her own and not even the promise of a career.

Dinner. We still have to eat. From the freezer at the top

of the fridge I pull out a bag of jumbo shrimp. I'll fry them in butter and garlic, serve them over rice with parsley from the herb garden out front. Cool water runs over my fingers into a bowl, slowly, so the sound of the stream doesn't obliterate Carl's voice. I cut open the bag of shrimp. The whole chunk barely fits in the bowl.

"We'll wait to hear from you, then," he says before he hangs up.

"You were rude to him."

"Who?"

"Hans."

"Let's not talk about it," he says. "Do you want to know what Rita said?"

"They don't know anything, do they?"

"Yes. They do."

Why does he do this? Why doesn't he just say what it is?

"Don't cry, my pet. She's fine. Sylvie called the place. She's in Ohio. She hitched a ride with a trucker and is waiting at a motel until someone from Douglas House can fly out there."

"How could she get all the way to Ohio? We should fly out ourselves. Carl?"

"What, my Jess?"

"I don't think I'm strong enough to go and get her."

"Of course you are. You are the strongest woman I know."

"No, Carl, you're strong. Should we go there? To Ohio? I've never been there."

"They'll take care of it. By the way, Rita said the boyfriend left, too."

"The boyfriend?"

"Apparently she really does have a boyfriend."

"Do you think he's a real boyfriend?"

"I don't know, my love."

"He's with her?"

"No. She's alone. They don't know where he is. Name is Ralph something or other."

"Carl? Why do you think we were chosen to have someone like Sylvie? I can't cope. Why can't she just get better? Pills. Or something. Why doesn't anything work?"

"I don't know the answers to these things. Do you think I always know what to do?"

"Yes, Carl, you do."

He did the first day Sylvie went crazy. It was just before her high school graduation. I suppose we should have seen it coming, but what do you look for? A sign popping out on her forehead that says SCHIZOPHRENIC? She'd always been a bit strange, with her little village on that braided rug and spending so much time in the tree and other things. Sometimes I'd hug her tight and she'd hug back but I could feel she wasn't all there, wasn't really hugging me, was embracing something else far away and bigger than me. Not a God or anything like that. Just something powerful in a distant place where I couldn't go.

My father was there and my brother, Harry, and his wife. Carl's family was all dead, of course, but he had invited a couple of the doctors he worked with to come because we were having a big barbecue afterward in celebration.

She was fine at breakfast. A little odd, but then she was

always a little odd. She picked at her omelet and when my father told her she'd need her energy for the graduation, she threw the fork against the wall, eggs flying everywhere. Dad told her to pick up the fork and asked what the hell was wrong with her, but of course Sylvie was beyond hearing any of that. "Sylvie," I said, "please pick up the fork." What a fool I was. As a cartoon moves on the screen, Sylvie meandered toward the thrown fork, muttering terrible words to herself. I was sorry I'd asked her to pick it up. Who gives a rat's ass about a fork on the floor? But Sylvie did.

Her limbs jerked in slow motion. She moved robotlike across the room and when she passed me she growled like an animal, deep in her throat. She bent and curled her fingers around the fork handle and stabbed the floor over and over and over until the tines bent into her palm. Even the blood didn't stop her stabbing. She laughed out loud. Dad was yelling. I stood helpless, terrified. Carl rushed to her, scooped her up, and held her very tight until she stopped. But after that she didn't speak when we asked how she was, and she didn't go to her graduation.

We tried everything for the next few days, but finally a week later, the doctor said we had no choice and had to admit her. She was slipping away from us. We went to the hospital to see her the next day, of course. She huddled in a corner, silent, face like stone. I saw the pain in her eyes. I stood there for what seemed like hours and she didn't move. I couldn't just leave her like that. I began to sway and move my arms in a dance, slowly, as close to her as I dared get. There was no response that day but I danced the next and the next. The fourth day, I brought a tape player and a cassette of music by Saint-Saëns and played "The Swan," and she rose with her arms spread and danced her swan until the swan died, picked herself up from the floor, and hugged me. "Mom, let me show you my room," she said. And a week later she was home.

"I'm a doctor," Carl says, "but that doesn't mean I'm God, now, does it?"

"Who is this boy? Did they say?"

"Ralph? No. I didn't ask. What does it matter?"

"Should one of us go out? To the store? We could use some milk. I don't think we should leave the phone, but you could go."

"No," he says. "I'll stay here. You go if you want."

"Did you hear that?"

"What? There's nothing, my pet," he says. "Just the wind and the gulls and maybe bears ready to get you and coyotes and—"

"Stop. You're teasing me."

He laughs. I love it when he laughs, which isn't often. People who've lived through a war have a hard time laughing.

"I'm going to the tree again. She might go there, you know. She might be lying about being in Ohio. And I'll get the yarn while I'm out."

"Why would she lie about that?"

When Carl stoops to pick up the paints and papers from the floor, he looks old to me. I pat his shoulder as I pass by. The air has chilled and I'm glad for the flashlight in my pocket because there is no moon and I might need it. In the distance, a pack of coyotes howls. I flick the light on and follow the beam toward the pine tree, and all the way there the howling goes on and on.

"Sylvie. Are you there?"

And what if she is?

Sometimes I dream about having a daughter who marries a nice man and has two children, a boy and a girl, who call me Nanny Jess and climb up on my lap while I read about dragons and fairies and ogres. I'm not sure that the boys want any children. Charlie's wife is a fancy lawyer and Sam isn't even married. Sylvie was pregnant once. It was years ago when we lived in Connecticut. She'd just moved into a group home when they called and asked if we knew who the father might be. I drove the two hours alone because Carl was operating on someone that day. I brought a picnic lunch so that Sylvie and I could talk in private. The conversation was simple. I asked who the father was. She said first that it was King Kong. Then it was Paul Newman. I don't think she had any idea who it was. I wanted a grandchild. Carl and I had talked about it and part of me wanted to take the child and raise it. I thought that it might bring Sylvie around if she had a baby to take care of. But I knew that was all a lie. I made her get the abortion.

Well, who would take care of a child born in a group home to a woman not capable? And I was truly too old even then to raise a child. After our picnic at the edge of a meadow of wildflowers, she laid her head on my lap while I brushed her hair with my palm and sang little songs, "Hush, Little Baby, Don't Say a Word" and "The Fox Went Out on a Chilly Night," as she moaned softly to herself. "Sylvie, raising a baby is hard. Let me help you. Daddy knows a good doctor."

The doctor was the wife of one of Carl's colleagues. Sylvie held my hand in the waiting room, dug at my thumb until she broke the skin. I murmured soothing words about its being the best thing and that she'd forget all about it in a while.

The whole procedure was short. Sylvie handled everything like a normal woman when they had her undress and climb onto the table. She didn't cry out or get angry, just did exactly as she was told.

"But Mommy, would you kill your child? Would you kill me? If you'd known?"

I didn't answer her. "After it's over, you and I will go to a hotel. Boston, perhaps. We'll watch movies and eat room service. We'll order shrimp and cheesecake. Won't that be fun?"

"No. It won't be fun." And she cried. I was never sure whether she cried for the baby or for herself. And there went my grandchild, flushed down the institutional toilet.

They wanted to sterilize her at the same time, but I wouldn't sign. I think she's on the pill now, just in case. That's a good thing, considering she has a boyfriend named Ralph.

At the tree I freeze and listen hard. There's no sound that is human. When I call out, no one answers. I shine the light up into the branches to see if the branch is still there. In the dark, with just a small shaft of light, the branch hangs at an odd angle. When it falls, I'll be sad. Isn't that a silly thing? To be attached to a broken branch? But it's Sylvie's solace, there in the crotch of that tree. When she was a small child, Carl climbed up with her and they pretended to be hiding from something bad. Now when Sylvie comes home, she still shinnies up to her spot, using stumps and holes in the bark for steps. What if she tries to climb onto the branch and it snaps?

The flashlight beam fades. The damn batteries are old. When I stop walking I listen hard for other footsteps or a rustling in the bushes. The coyotes have stopped their eerie racket and the only sounds are small noises in dry leaves, squirrels perhaps, or birds. Carl's right. Sylvie isn't here. How could she get here? But then, how could she get to Ohio?

# 5

## JESSIE

WHEN I APPROACH the house, all the lights are lit like some brazen Christmas display. I hate Christmas, especially the colored lights all over the lawns around here and the loud music in the stores.

My childhood Christmases were days of wishing our mother wasn't dead. Our father sat in his wingback chair, smoking and drinking sherry until tears slipped down his face and he gathered Harry and me onto his lap to tell us that it wasn't our fault, that we were just babies, and that our mother died because she was too small and we were too big. Too big to come out. My aunts and my grandmother always came for dinner or we went there in the evening for roast beef and Yorkshire pudding. But through the day we both felt much too big.

I flick off the almost-dead flashlight and step carefully over exposed roots and stones around the back of the house toward the garage.

We really need a new car. The side panels are beginning to rust from all the winter salt. The back door sticks and creaks when I open it. The blasted interior light is broken and the flashlight is dim when I push the on button, but it throws enough light for me to see the paper bag full of yarn on the floor of the backseat. It's all there. The Donegal tweed and the primaries for socks.

I glance up the driveway but the dusk impairs my vision. And the damn broken glasses. There's no one there. No one that I can see, anyway. We don't really need milk. How foolish. I grab the bag of yarn and go back into the house. I think Carl is secretly afraid of the dark and that's why he turns on all the lights.

I smell smoke coming out of the chimney. He must have started a fire in the woodstove. When I go back into the house, Carl isn't talking on the telephone.

He watches me as I hang up my parka, pull off my scarf, turn off the ceiling light, and pour myself a glass of red wine.

"Do you want one?"

He doesn't answer me, but I pour a second glass and bring it to the table after I light a candle. Carl flicks off most of the lights. I'm afraid to ask if anyone's called. I sip my wine. Carl sips his.

"Was she in the tree?"

I don't answer the question.

"She called again."

"What?"

"She called. She isn't in Ohio."

"Why didn't you say someone called? And how could

she be in Ohio? It's too far. Where is she? Why did you ask if she was in the tree?"

"She wouldn't say where she was, but I've called Douglas House. Someone's already flown to Columbus."

"Shit," I say. Between us on the table are my glasses, fixed. I put them on without speaking of them. Carl fixes things. Everything. So why the hell can't he fix his daughter?

We sit in silence and near darkness sipping our wine while the cold shrimp drain in the sink. How could we have kept her at home? I can't cope with her when she freaks out. And it's not safe.

"I'm hungry," he says. "Shall I cook up the shrimp?"

"How can you think of food right now? What is Sylvie eating? Garbage from the back of a Dumpster?"

Not all our times with Sylvie have been difficult. When she was fifteen we built this house to replace the old cottage that she burned down. It was a mistake, of course, an accident. She was just trying to make smoke to hide in. That's what she said. I have to believe her. I know it doesn't make sense, but it made sense to her.

We ordered all the materials from the building supply place to be delivered to the site and invited everyone we knew for a weekend of hammering and sawing and eating lobsters. Our old friend Jacob, from down the road, was the contractor and head carpenter. He died last year. He had the plans and knew how to execute them. We all had a job. Mine was cooking and putting up sheathing. Carl did framing with the boys. Even my father came and worked on running wires and plumbing with the people we hired. But the best was Harry. He pulled up his lawn chair close to the activity and directed everything. He had lists of things to be done and gave Sylvie little bits of paper to hand out to the workers with their instructions. They sat close together and murmured about little changes that would make the house cozier or brighter or warmer. In a way, they were both damaged people, maimed in some way. Sylvie in her mind and Harry in his hip. Why do we expect that all human beings should be perfect? That day, Sylvie and Harry together, their foreheads touching while he wrote out the instructions for building our house, were perfect.

And together, they hypnotized thirty-seven lobsters before they went into the pots, just to give them a quick and painless death. That weekend we essentially built a house. Of course, there was lots of work to do after that, especially on the inside, but at the end of the weekend, a house stood where there had been none.

I don't realize I'm standing until Carl's hand on my forearm tugs me back down into my chair. All I want to do is paint in the woods and read my books and watch the birds on their rocks. But I can't because Sylvie is missing.

"You sit here and listen," he says. He scans the radio dial until he finds chamber music on public radio. He thinks it will relax me. As if there is something wrong with me. As if I'm the one needing repair. "I'll fix the shrimp," he says. "Garlic? Rice? Parsley?"

While he chops garlic, gathers parsley, steams rice, I knit, hoping that I don't reach the heel before supper is ready. The socks were going to be for me but now I think I'll give them to Sylvie for Christmas. She loves stripes. I'll knit the toe red.

Carl sings again. Not children's songs this time, but old songs in a minor key, no words, just "la-la" and "do-do-do," just so you know the tune. I hear the butter bubble up and the wet shrimp sizzle as he dumps them from the colander into the frying pan just before the knock on the door. Sylvie? Or Hans again? There was no headlight or engine noise. Hans doesn't like to walk the path in the darkness. It must be Sylvie. I drop the sock onto the table and rush past Carl, knocking the bowl of parsley to the floor.

Even before I open the door I'm ready with my arms to embrace her. When I see the man, my arms drop to my sides, empty of their mission. He is handsome there on the stoop, slapping his arms to keep warm, a lock of blond hair falling over his eyes. He grins like a child when he sees me.

"Rather silly, I know," he says. "My gear. It got stolen."

"Stolen?"

"My camping gear. I saw your light. I'm not one to intrude but I'm not sure where I am and it's dark and everything is gone. All my gear."

He hugs himself and tilts his head, raises his brow like Charlie does when he feels sheepish. "I have two boys," I say. I feel Carl behind me wondering why I would say such a thing.

"What's the problem, young man?" Carl asks.

"As I said, sir, someone stole my stuff. Sleeping bag, tent, food, map, flashlight."

"How could someone steal your gear? You go off and leave it?"

"For heaven's sake, Carl, can't you see he's cold and hungry?"

"Cold? He's wearing a jacket. Why would he be cold?"

"Well, hungry, then."

"The jacket is my dad's. Thank God that didn't get stolen."

"What's your name?"

"Jonah, sir."

"Have you been in the woods?" I ask. "Near the old pine tree?"

"Been walking close to the shore, looking for house lights. Saw lots of pine trees. I'm willing to pitch in for a place to stay the night."

"Are you hungry?" I ask. I'm aware of Carl. He doesn't want the man in the house. Jonah's polite. And young. And cold. And what a nice name. "It really isn't a good time," I say.

"Oh?"

"Have you notified the police?" Carl asks.

"It just happened," Jonah says. "I haven't had a chance. Perhaps I could use your phone."

He blows warm air into his palms, licks the corner of his mouth. He's not dressed warmly enough, although he does wear a jacket. No scarf. No hat. And the air is cooling off.

"The main road is just up the driveway," Carl says. "Ten minutes' walk if you walk fast."

"I can split wood," he says. "I'm a pretty good cook."

"Carl?" I say, not really to Carl.

"We have that pile of maple to split," Carl says. "But we don't really need it right now."

"I'd be glad to. I know it's an intrusion and you don't even know me. But. Well. I'm stuck."

"Why don't you go around back to the car," Carl says. "I'll drive you to the highway."

"They've taken my money," Jonah says. "Everything."

"It'll be easier in the daylight," I say.

"My mom can pick me up tomorrow. She's scared to drive at night and she's a couple of hours away. Besides, she isn't home now."

"You shouldn't be camping alone," I say.

"Just what my mom said," he says. "'Find a friend,' she said, 'so you won't be out there all alone.'"

"Well, then," I say. "Come on. We'll figure something out."

"Jess," Carl says. That's all. Just "Jess."

Jonah doesn't wait for me to ask him. He steps into the house and closes the door behind him. "Nice place," he says.

"Do you like shrimp?" I ask.

"You're so kind," he says. "You must know how it is to worry about your children."

"Yes. We do."

"He could fill the wood box after he makes the call," Carl says.

"Sure. Where's the pile?"

"Come in and eat first," I say.

"What about the call?" Carl asks.

"Oh, let's eat first," I say. "The dinner's getting cold."

Carl pours the shrimp over a platter of rice and sprinkles chopped parsley over the top. We don't have a salad tonight. Or bread. Just the one platter on the table looks sparse. Carl sets a plate on the long side of the table, between us, then a napkin, a water glass, a fork. He pours me another glass of wine, pours Jonah a glass of water. Is he too young to drink? He looks about twenty-five. I watch his hands grip the fork, bring a shrimp to his mouth. His fingers are slim, uncallused. I wonder if he is truly a seasoned camper or whether this is a whim, a fancy, something he's always wanted to do. Perhaps he's a student. Yes. That's it.

Carl asks first. Jonah says he's in graduate school, studying to be an ornithologist. I ask him about the gulls and why they face the sun. He laughs and says it's an old wives' tale. I don't tell him that I see it from my window every morning while I have my tea and in the evening while I wait for the sun to disappear. His teeth are very straight but his eyes are bloodshot and his stubble is several days old. Should I offer to let him shave and take a shower? Hard to keep clean when you're camping. He keeps his jacket on. Says he's more comfortable.

He holds a shrimp in his mouth, tail sticking out through his closed lips, and hums. Not a tune. Just a noise. I think, for a moment, of Sylvie and the way she hums sometimes when she chews. Jonah sees me watching and stops. I stir my few remaining grains of rice around on my plate just to have something to do.

"Isn't it time to call the police?" Carl asks.

He pulls the pink tail from his lips and places it on the edge of his plate. "Yes. Sure," he says. "Tomorrow."

"We haven't talked about tomorrow," Carl says.

# 6

## JESSIE

"No," CARL SAYS. "Perhaps you should call now."

"Carl, let him finish his dinner."

"He's finished," Carl says. "You're finished, aren't you?"

"Yes," he says. "I'll call."

It's impossible not to listen to a conversation when you're within hearing distance of it. When Carl points in the direction of the telephone, the boy sidles toward it and sits right down in my knitting chair. Carl talks about nothing and I nod at the appropriate times. I pour him some more wine so he will stop talking over Jonah's conversation. I gaze out the black window into nothing, pick up the few remaining grains of rice between the tines of my fork.

"I just went for a five-minute walk," Jonah says into the receiver. "When I came back, everything was gone."

There is a pause. Carl begins to speak again. I rest my fingers on his hand, say, "Have your wine, dear."

I don't think Carl is fooled. He knows me. But he sips quietly and allows me the silence.

"Sure. Thanks. Some nice folks have invited me to dinner. I'm sure I can spend the night here."

Carl raises his eyebrows at that one. But what is the boy to do? We have a guest room upstairs and the downstairs couch opens up. In Connecticut when Carl was replacing hips and knees, young residents often stayed over. They would chat well into the night over a glass of wine about new surgical techniques and favorite prosthetic models. We didn't know much about their backgrounds, either. But what if Sylvie calls? I don't want to have to explain anything to a complete stranger.

Jonah is just hanging up when I hear a car pulling into the driveway and then the muffled sound of a car door closing. It's Hans again with Marte. Marte doesn't limp at all.

"We went out to Dunlap's for lobster and felt like a game of Scrabble," Hans says. "Well, who's this chap?"

Before Carl has a chance to say the wrong thing, I jump in. "Jonah. His camping gear was stolen. We gave him dinner."

"Well, what do you say about Scrabble, Carl?"

Is it that Hans is stupid, or is he just impervious to Carl's dislike of him? Perhaps he doesn't really care. Perhaps his desire to play Scrabble is more important than his own ego. Carl's like that, too.

"Go ahead, folks," Jonah says. "I'll clean up here. That's the least I can do." He simply begins clearing plates, glasses, silverware, filling the sink, without instruction. Strange that he should be so comfortable in someone else's kitchen.

Hans pulls the other end of the kitchen table out from

the window. Marte slides a fourth chair behind the table. I sit on the outside in case the telephone rings.

"Hans said you have troubles with your dear Sylvie again, so we've come to keep your mind off things," Marte says.

"Not really troubles," I say. "She's off on a small trip. We just aren't sure where. I'm sure she's fine. She's an adult, after all."

Carl pulls the Scrabble game from the shelf and opens the board on the table. He loves Scrabble. It's the only reason he's tolerating Hans.

"Who is Sylvie?" asks Jonah.

"Sylvie's the daughter," Hans says.

"But that isn't really any concern of yours," says Carl.

"Just asking."

Jonah does a good job on the dishes. From my seat I can watch him. His face behind the stubble is classic handsome and his skin is flawless, smooth and unblemished, as if he had never been in the sun. When he reaches to put the wineglasses away, his jeans expose skin where his underwear should be. I don't think he's wearing any at all. The jacket seems a little small for him. It's an expensive jacket. Wool. Handwoven, perhaps. Blue and green stripes. Very subtle. Not really a camping jacket.

"I'm sorry," he says. "Where are my manners? There's a half a bottle of red wine left. Would anyone like some?"

"Young man," Carl says, "that's our—"

"Sure," says Hans. "Love some. How about you, Jessie? You look like you could use some, and Marte's leg could use some numbing, couldn't it, dear?"

Jonah pours the rest of the wine among four glasses and hands them out while Hans readies the board. We pick our letters. My mind struggles to keep everything separate— the telephone, the strange man, the letters that don't go together to make up any word at all.

"I see you're working on another sock," Marte says.

"Is it for Sylvie?" Jonah asks.

I drop my letter onto the center of the board. The word. What was my word? Marte turns my letter over. It's an *S*. I reach for my glass and sip the dark red burgundy slowly while I think. Jonah doesn't seem to notice that I don't answer his question. He puts away the dishes.

After he wipes the counters, he pulls up a chair beside me. When he leans to point to the *T*, his arm brushes my hand. *Starch.* That's it. My word. I place the small wooden tiles on the board, line them up with Carl's *H*, then sit back satisfied.

"Well, is it?" asks Marte.

"What?"

"The sock. Is it for Sylvie?"

"No. I don't know."

"When you finish those dishes," Carl says, "you'd better get along. It's only a mile to the road. You'll catch a ride there."

"You're going to send him out in the dark with nothing?" asks Hans.

"We don't know who he is," says Carl. "We don't know anything about him."

And all this time, Jonah sits at the table with us, looking from one to the other as they speak about him as if he weren't there. The telephone rings.

"Shall I get that?" Jonah says.

"No. No," I say. "Don't touch the telephone." But he is younger and more agile than I. When I clutch the receiver he releases it to me, but I don't think he wants to.

"Hello? Hello? Is someone there?"

They all watch me, waiting to know. Laughter. That's what I hear. Sylvie's laughter. I can't speak until I walk around the corner, away from their stares.

"Sylvie? It's Mommy." I try to speak softly just because this isn't for the whole world. "Where are you?"

"In a phone booth."

"Are you all right?"

"Of course I'm all right. Do you think I'm a child?"

"No. You're not a child. Where are you?"

"*I'm in the fucking zoo! In the monkey cage!*"

"Hans and Marte are here playing Scrabble, but I can come and get you. Are you close by? Please, Sylvie."

She doesn't answer, doesn't tell me anything. Carl takes the phone.

"Sylvie? Answer me. Where are you?" His voice is loud. They're all listening. Sylvie's screaming is loud enough to be heard throughout the room, especially when Carl holds the receiver out from his ear. I take it from him.

"None of your business," she says. "None of your business."

"Sylvie, you need your medicine. Do you have your medicine?"

The screaming stops but I don't think it has anything to do with the medicine. "I have a boyfriend," she says. "He's beautiful."

"Do you, dear? What's his name?"

"Ralph. He loves me. He really does. I'm going back because he's there. I don't know why I left. Mom? Are you there?"

"I'm making you some socks for Christmas."

"He isn't going to be there long. He's leaving, too. He wants me to leave with him, get a job, an apartment. Do you think I can do it, Mom?"

"Of course you can. I'll give you some furniture from the old house. It's still in storage."

"Do you have a bed?"

"Your old bed needs a mattress. Daddy's and mine does, too, I think. We went painting today. And a young man stopped in here. He was camping and his gear was stolen. He stayed for supper."

"What does he look like? Is he beautiful? Does he love me?" And then she hangs up. I hold the receiver to my ear until an electronic voice says, "Please hang up and try again." They all think we're still talking and I don't know how to end the conversation. Jonah steps forward as if he wants to take the phone.

"Well, lovely to talk to you, dear. We'll see you at Thanksgiving." What can I do? Carl knows. He knows everything. Hans and Marte pretend to study their letters, glance back and forth from the board to their letter stand. Carl moves close, offers his hand to me. And Jonah glares at me. What have I done? Who is he? Does he know something? Does he know Sylvie? He's not just a camper who's been robbed, is he?

# 7

## CARL

JESSIE'S RIGHT. I've never been able to fix Sylvie. You'd think with all my medical training I'd be able to fix anything if I tried hard enough, and God knows with my daughter I've tried everything. Sometimes she's right there, but more often than not she is somewhere else where sane people can't go, like Never-Never-Land. I read somewhere that many psychotics describe an identical crazy world and voices that use the same words. How could people who don't even know one another come up with the same crazy place? It makes me wonder if it is a real world where only the privileged few are allowed and doctors who fix bones are not among them.

This boy who's barged his way into our house could probably go there, to that place. He's most likely harmless but there's something about him that makes me uneasy, like the way he's looking at Jessie. Almost as if he knows us and hates us. But he doesn't know us. He reminds me a little of myself at that age. Angry about the war. Enraged at the Germans. So enraged that I couldn't even concentrate on my studies. But that's behind me. We move on.

"Come on, Jess," I say. She's unsteady and if it weren't for Hans and Marte and Jonah watching, she'd be sobbing about Sylvie and angry at me for not making things better. If I embrace her she will break down. I have to help her be strong. "Let's finish the game."

Is it because I'm so large that people seem to listen to me? Jonah backs off and resumes fussing with the counters. Jessie returns to her seat, picks up five letters from the up-turned pile, lines them up on her holder.

Hans plays next. His fingers are milky white, delicate, the fingers of a man who does nothing. I remember hands like that in the camp, hands that did nothing but fill gloves and tap a riding crop on an upturned palm. He's retired from something scientific but I've never talked to him about it. I think he was an oculist. His voice has just a trace of an accent, but Marte's is still strong. He wouldn't have been quite old enough to have worked in the camp or been in the army. He would have been a child, like me. His word is *tattoo*, crossing the *T* of Jessie's *starch*.

"Hey, isn't that a tattoo on your arm?" Jonah asks.

"Yes, I often wondered about that," Hans says. "You don't seem the type for a tattoo. Did you get that in the service?"

"Just something I picked up in my youth."

"What is it?" Hans asks.

"A fish," I say. "Had it done one night after a bit too

much beer. Just an impulsive kid thing." I tug my sweatshirt sleeve down to my wrist.

When Marte begs off because of a headache, Jonah takes her place at the Scrabble board. His mind is sharp. He makes words like *wadmal* and *zeatin* and we have to look them up in the dictionary to make sure they're really words. Is that what he does, study words?

When Jonah excuses himself to use the bathroom, Hans says there's something very weird about the boy, but he reminds me of some of the young interns who worked with me at the hospital: clever, astute, full of facts but a bit naive.

"I once heard eagles mate in the air. Is that true?" I ask when he returns. After all, he says he's an ornithologist.

"Carl," Jessie says. "What a question."

"Actually," Jonah says, "that's a fascinating question. In fact, they are the only bird that mates in the air."

"Oh, really?" Jessie says. She has calmed down. She tends to overreact to some things. The uneasiness she has felt since Jonah's glare upset her earlier is replaced with a sincerity and confidence, but I'm not sure that it's true about the eagles. I heard it somewhere, but it seems preposterous that those huge birds mate without something to push against. I'm going to look that up in the bird book after he leaves.

"Where are you going with all this knowledge?" I ask. "What do you want to do with it?"

"Research on endangered birds, I think. Especially ducks. Do you know the harlequin? That's what I'm looking for. I've heard they've been seen near here."

"Do they look like a clown?"

"They do, in fact. Give me a piece of paper and some markers or crayons. I'll draw one."

"But the game isn't finished," Hans says.

Jonah follows me to the chest where we keep our painting supplies. I hand him a sketch pad and a package of colored pencils.

"What's that?" he asks.

"Just a tree. A pine tree."

"Why so many paintings of a tree?"

"I like trees."

Jonah's audacity intrigues me. His social skills are lacking but he's bright. Jessie might call him sassy.

Back at the table, he draws a squat duck with a ringed neck and white head spots. "There it is. Ever see one?"

"No," Jessie says. "Not like that." She's fine now. There is no sign of hysteria about Sylvie. The young man seems just a tad eccentric but many intelligent people are a bit odd. The poor kid. Sometimes I wonder why I'm so rude and insensitive to people.

"How about it, Carl?" Jonah says. "Have you got a spot on that couch for my poor bod? I'll be leaving first thing in the morning. Check out the police station. Well, what do you say?"

"Well, I suppose that's the least I could do," I say.

"What's the least you could do, Carl?" Jonah asks.

"Let you sleep on the couch," I say. "I'll think about it."

Hans and Marte seem surprised I even entertained the thought, but they don't speak up. I wouldn't put up with them if it weren't for Jessie. She needs friends. Hans and Marte make leaving noises, say that Marte needs her sleep because she has to head out early tomorrow. Hans says maybe he'll drop by. I'm glad to see them go but I should have asked them to drive the boy to the top of the hill. I would have if Hans hadn't commented on how mean I was.

"Mr. Jensen," Jonah says, "I truly appreciate your letting me stay."

"That's Dr. Jensen, and I said you could have dinner. Not spend the night."

"I beg to differ," Jonah says. "You clearly invited me for the night."

"Carl, the boy doesn't even have a hat. Remember Sam when he hitched to Alabama and people put him up?"

"Jess, we don't know this boy."

"And what of Sylvie? Is someone letting her sleep on their couch?"

"There's a tent in the garage, isn't there, Jess?"

"Don't be such a curmudgeon," she says.

"I'll split that wood after breakfast and I'll be gone."

Jonah asks for videos. He says he has a hard time falling asleep in a strange place. Jessie pulls out what few videos we have: *The Piano, Thelma & Louise, Fried Green Tomatoes, Sophie's Choice,* all women's movies. I don't watch movies very often. I apologize for the selection, but he says they're fine, that he'll keep the sound turned down so as not to bother our sleep.

She goes upstairs and I notice she looks behind her for the dog that's been dead for weeks. Jonah watches while I maneuver the pillow down from the top shelf in the closet and choose a couple of warm wool blankets from the basket on the floor.

"Wow. You play the violin?"

"Not anymore. A long time ago. In another life."

"Looks like no one's played it for years. That's too bad. What happened to the bridge? And the neck looks a little warped. Looks like it's been around." Jonah reaches for the violin.

"Please leave it alone," I say.

"I used to play violin. Suzuki. When I was little. And then the youth orchestra. What did you play? Classical? Bluegrass?"

"I told you. I don't play anymore."

"But what did you play when you played?"

"Just little tunes. It's late. I'm going up."

Did I really invite him to stay? Why did I do that? Is it too late to throw him out? Jessie would have a fit. I don't offer him anything to sleep in. My pajamas are too big, and besides, young people don't wear pajamas anymore. When I climb the stairs I hear him rustling around with the blankets, popping the video box open, slipping the movie into the VCR. And somewhere inside me there is a dread that I haven't felt since the war and I don't know what to do with it.

Jessie is asleep. She's an angel. Her hair feathers over the pillow like gray corn silk. This is the only time I see her hair loose, and it reminds me of my mother's hair. When we arrived at the camp her hair was dark as a moonless night, but it turned gray, actually almost white. We were allowed to keep our hair. Isn't that strange? The others we could see over the fence had their heads shaved but families on our block didn't. When we were made to remove our clothes, the women tried to hide their nakedness with their hair, but of course that was futile. My grandmother tried. She held strands of silver hair over her flapping breasts when they took her. She couldn't look at us. She was too ashamed. Many of us had our hair turn from black to white in a short period of time. Even some of the young women.

I kiss Jessie's forehead and she stirs. I undress in the near dark, the only light coming from the downstairs television. My pajamas are somewhere on the floor where I dropped them this morning. Was it only this morning? The day seems long. Was it just today Jessie made the smoked salmon omelet? The pajamas are nowhere. Then I notice them folded on my pillow. Jessie. When I reach for them, the fish on my arm glimmers as if it had real scales. What kind of a fish is it? I don't know. I just told them to cover up what was there with something else. Something peaceful. No lions or skulls. No naked women. They chose a fish. Just some kind of fish. It doesn't matter what kind it is.

She turns toward me when I lower myself into the bed. Her mouth moves in sleep, making me wonder about her dream. I bring her close to me until her breath warms my neck. The television drones on and on. Should I go down and ask him to switch it off? We turn in our bed, toward each other, away from each other, together. Jessie sleeps like a child except that every once in a while she snorts or hums and I think she is dreaming of our daughter.

Sylvie was the most enchanting child. "Popsie," she called me. If she weren't ill, she could be a model or a leading lady or a dancer. I used to imagine that she came from the woods, even before she was born. That's why I named her Sylvie, for the forest. A sprite. An elf. A fairy. She loved the pine tree. She still does. I think it's because she can hide there in the safe spot where the large branch juts from the trunk. Now it has that crack. We'll probably lose it in the next storm.

"Giddyap, Popsie," she said. "To the magic tree. Faster."

She rode on my shoulders, long legs dangling on my chest while she held fast around my neck and kicked her feet on my ribs. It was a game we played. We'd leave the boys with Jessie and spend the morning in the woods. In those days we only spent a few weeks up here every summer in the little cabin, which is long gone.

"Come on, Popsie, you come up, too."

"I'm too big to climb trees."

"But I'll be all alone up here and they'll get you."

"Who, little sprite? There's no one here."

She perched on the lowest limb with her arms spread out and begged me to climb, to get away from them, to be safe. I should have realized something then. But aren't all kids scared of the boogeyman?

"Look, Pops, there. And there. Behind the rock. They're coming. The tree will protect us."

"OK. I'll try." And I'd climb. Me. Big, bulky me. It wasn't really difficult because there were stubs of branches we'd thinned that made perfect steps. At the crotch was a hollowed-out place where we stored our cookies and juice.

We covered it with an old plastic dishpan to keep it dry. And there we'd sit for a long time, our legs hanging down, watching for intruders. Once, we sat so still that a doe browsed with her fawns right underneath us until Sylvie sneezed. I haven't climbed that tree in years.

Jonah finishes *Thelma & Louise* and I picture the soar into the Grand Canyon. He gets up from the couch. I can hear the springs creak. Another video goes into the VCR. It's *Sophie's Choice*. I know because of the music.

The clock reads almost two. I consider shutting the bedroom door but I don't feel comfortable with the door shut. And besides, I want to know what is going on downstairs. I hear the dialogue, the piano music, and occasional hushed comments from Jonah, and I wish he would fall asleep. I pad over to the door and swing it toward the jamb. Not shut tight. Ajar enough for me to hear movement.

My hand slips underneath Jessie's nightgown to her breasts, where it is warm and slightly damp. When she was young they were hard, dense, but now they rest like empty silk sacks in my palm. When Sylvie was born, Jessie had a hard time nursing because she was so full, breasts hard as tennis balls, but she kept at it. When Sylvie was just a week old, I came home from the hospital to find Jessie sitting in the living room in a straight-backed chair, sobbing quietly while Sylvie sucked at her. I guided her to the rocker, folded a warm facecloth on her forehead, sang a little song. And there we sat while Sylvie nursed for the first time with vigor until Jessie's breasts were almost emptied. She didn't wean her until she was pregnant with Charlie.

Sylvie was two and a half. Was that the first sign of trouble? Jessie's obstetrician said we must wean her right away. "Do it 'cold turkey,'" he'd said. "Just stop. Tell her no." Sylvie screamed until a neighbor came over to see if there was a problem. Jessie went to her sister's, over an hour away, and left me with Sylvie for the weekend. When she came back, Sylvie was weaned. When Charlie was finally born, Sylvie ignored him and we thought that was better than being jealous.

Now I knew it was a mistake, sending Jessie away like that, her breasts swollen and sore. We should never have listened to the doctor. It was too hard on her, leaving Sylvie. Jessie did her best with the children, and Charlie and Sam are good men, successful, kind. But I know she aches for Sylvie. Sometimes I think she believes that Sylvie will come out of it, have a husband, children, give us grandchildren.

Rain pings on our metal roof. That's why we went with the metal. We both love the rain and the sound it makes. It blots out most of the noise of the television and the sound of Jonah's utterances.

Jessie presses against me and asks if I am asleep. I tell her that I am, indeed, sound asleep. She turns and slides her arms around me.

"Is it going to be all right?"

"Yes, my pet. It is."

# 8

## JESSIE

I HEAR CARL RUSTLING around in the near dark searching for his pajamas and wonder how long it will take for him to notice that I've folded them on his pillow. That man, Jonah, is still watching a movie and it's the middle of the night, for God's sake. And the telephone is silent. Where is Sylvie sleeping? In a shelter? A Dumpster? In a motel room with someone she just met? With Ralph? Or is Ralph here? To-morrow I'm going to ask him.

Carl mutters something when he finds the pajamas. Why is it taking him so long to get into bed? When he finally pulls the covers back and slides in beside me, I nestle close to him. His body makes me feel warm and protected. When I awake again, music from *The Piano* makes me wonder for a moment where I am. Carl's hand is under my nightgown and he's holding my breasts. It's raining onto the metal roof and we're both awake. I turn toward him.

"Is it going to be all right?" I ask.

"Yes, my pet," he says. "It is."

He kisses my hair and murmurs something I can't hear. When he pulls me hard against him, I smell his scent, the scent that allows blindfolded mothers to find their children. I imagine that when he's gone, I'll sleep with his pajamas on my pillow. I loosen the tie around his waist until my hand slides down his smooth skin. When he pushes my nightgown up, we press against each other and he tells me he loves me. Why do we say that after forty years? I don't know.

He rolls on top of me and opens me. Charlie was shocked that we still do this. I don't remember how the subject came up but it was at some holiday dinner. Charlie said, "Mom? Dad?" looking from one to the other. "Really?" he said. He chuckled and patted my hand but I think he was horrified.

When Carl goes into me, I feel safe, not excited. Safe. After it's finished, he stays in me while we fall asleep. I don't sleep well. Each time I awaken, I find Carl sitting up in bed alert. The sound of videos from downstairs continues through the night but I have to strain to hear it.

When I finally wake up to the sunrise, Carl's side of the bed is empty and cold and there's no sound, no rain on the roof, no movie noise. My nightgown is pushed up around my waist. It's been a long time since we made love with anyone else in the house.

Yesterday I woke up thinking about what I wanted to paint, and today I think of Sylvie and wonder why the phone has been silent all night. Perhaps that's good. And the strange boy, Jonah. I'll ask him this morning if he knows her.

I'll finish that sock and start another today. When Sylvie

comes for Christmas, we'll knit together. She wants to learn to turn a heel. We'll light a fire in the new woodstove and sit at the window watching the ice heave against itself along the shore and the ospreys steal fish from eagles, and we'll knit while we talk about our lives. Perhaps she'll tell me about Ralph. Perhaps he's a lovely man who's been through some trauma and is recovering. Or perhaps he's Jonah.

Sylvie, the old Sylvie, lies somewhere underneath all the layers of craziness. It's just a matter of digging her out. I've read that sometimes mentally ill people return to their old selves suddenly, without warning, and lead productive lives. This Ralph may be just the thing. One moment I hope she is with him, and the next I don't. He can take care of her, make sure she doesn't get hurt. She's never had a serious relationship with a man before but she says Ralph loves her. Sylvie would love her children if she had them. *Please, God, let him be a good man.* Sometimes I say things like *Please, God* this and *Please, God* that, but there isn't really any God. It makes me feel safe to say the words. Isn't that crazy?

On the way down the stairs I hear breakfast sounds. The seldom-used coffeepot blurps on the gas burner, and the toaster pops. They sit at the table, Jonah in my place. Why didn't Carl ask him to sit in the other seat? Jonah appears disheveled and his hand bounces staccato-like on the table. Carl meets me by the stove, kisses my neck, says, "Good morning, my pet," and I'm glad Jonah isn't watching. That's kind of a private thing, isn't it?

He's filled the teakettle too full again and the water is still tepid. I put it back on the flaming burner to boil.

"Did you sleep at all?" I ask Jonah.

"Not much," he says.

"How were the videos?"

For the first time this morning, I see his face. It's younger than it was yesterday, or perhaps it's the morning light. His eyelids droop from lack of sleep but there's a kindness that I hadn't noticed before, an old-soul look to him. His tongue flicks at the edges of his mouth as if food is stuck there, and his T-shirt is old, faded. I notice his wool jacket draped over the arm of the couch.

"Do you have others?" he asks.

"Others?"

"Videos."

"No. Not many. A few old family movies. A couple of documentaries. *Planet of the Apes.*" Why would he want to know?

I do morning things. Check the answering machine just in case we didn't hear the ring. Lift the receiver of the telephone, just to check. There are two melons left in the fridge. I cut them both in half, scoop out the seeds, slice the halves into sections, and place them on a Blue Willow platter in the center of the table. A perfect still life, the orange flesh of the melons scattered over the deep blue figures against the background of the yellow table. It's perfect. Carl has set three place mats with small plates and knives to butter the bagels.

When I pass Jonah the spoon for his melon, we touch. I feel an excitement between us, a bond of some kind. It's just because he's so good looking, provocative, intriguing. When you get old, a bit of that memory of lusty youth keeps you going. That's why I love to daydream. Sometimes Carl and I tell each other our dreams while we lie together upstairs, just for fun. Carl was one of my first lovers, so I figure I owe myself a few fantasies.

"Coffee ready?" Jonah asks.

"I'll get it," I say. "Cream? Sugar?"

"No. Nothing. Black."

"Did you hear the telephone during the night?"

"Not a sound," he says.

"Did you see all the bird books? On the shelf?"

"No."

"Why do gulls face the sun?"

"You asked me that yesterday," he says.

"I'm sorry," I say.

The three of us sit at the table, eating ripe cantaloupe while the morning sun exposes dust drifting across the room. My seagulls stand one-legged in the wind, their feathery bottoms tilted up toward us. Jonah doesn't speak but his hand has ceased its tapping and is now gripping a hot cup of coffee. The only sounds come from eating and drinking. Carl and I usually chat at breakfast. When I look at him he seems bewildered by Jonah's taciturn manner.

"Are you tired?" I ask.

"No."

"Would you like to call your mother to pick you up now?"

"No. Not yet. She'll be sleeping."

"Another bagel?"

"I'd like to go to the tree," he says. "The pine tree in the painting."

"Why would you want to do that?" Carl asks.

"To prepare the way."

"What?" Carl asks. "Prepare what way?"

"Did Sylvie climb that tree?" Jonah asks. "Did she?"

Why does he ask? I glance at Carl. Yes. He wonders, too.

"I don't mean to pry," Jonah says. "I'm just curious."

His leg jiggles under the table and he sips his coffee. He's eaten most of the melon slices. He piles one empty skin segment onto the other as if he's building a structure of some kind.

"Where's your home?" I ask.

"My home is where the heart is."

"And where is that?"

"Wherever I am."

"Your parents?"

"Dead."

"But I thought—"

"Jonah and I were discussing the ethics of human cloning," Carl says. "Weren't we, Jonah?"

"Yes, Carl. We were."

"He says widespread use is inevitable and it's too late for laws to stop it."

"Like what if there were two Sylvies? Would they both be as lovely? Would you cherish them equally?"

"How do you know Sylvie is lovely?" I ask.

"Pictures. All over the house. And what if there were two Stalins? Two Hitlers?"

"You know her, don't you?" I ask.

"Your daughter? Why would you think that?"

"Well, it just seemed as if you might."

When Jonah leaves the table to get more coffee, I catch Carl's attention. I'm worried, but Carl reassures me with his eyes. But something isn't right.

"What's under the fish, Carl?"

"The fish?" Carl asks. His voice is thin.

Jonah steadies his steaming coffee in one hand, runs his other hand through his tousled hair. No one asks Carl about the fish. It's just one of those things, like the emperor's clothes. One of Carl's residents asked me about it once because he'd noticed it when Carl was operating. Kind of hard to miss, the boy'd said. Something he got as a teenager, I told him. And that was that. I knew there were numbers under the fish. The *Z* was clear through the blue eye, and the last number, *3*, protruded from the notch in the tail. I didn't have to ask. I just knew. Like Carl's scarred back, all crisscrossed like that. Someone did that to him. He didn't need to tell me. Of course, I knew he was in a camp. But some things are better left alone, buried in the past as they should be.

I find it difficult to look at Carl because I know what I'll see in his eyes, the embarrassment, the fear.

"Did they do that to you, Carl?" Jonah jolts the table when he paces by, spills his hot coffee over his hand. "Shit. The fucking coffee's hot. Did it hurt, Carl? The needle? What else did they do, Carl? Is Sylvie yours? From your sperm? Didn't they mess with you down there, too?"

I can't do anything but look at my plate. Carl's anger fills the kitchen but Jonah doesn't seem to notice it. What can I do? What can I say? I don't think the boy will harm me but I'm afraid anyway. Should I stand up? As he paces back and forth, drips from the coffee cup spatter the floor. He's young. Twenty-five. Maybe thirty. He shoves his hand in his jeans pocket and pops something in his mouth, swigs it down with the hot coffee. How could I have been attracted to him? What happened to his old soul? I think we've got to get him out of here.

"Burned my tongue," he says. "Now then." He sits down at the table and looks at us. "I guess that wasn't any of my business, was it?"

"No," Carl says. "It wasn't."

Tears pool up behind my eyes and I struggle to keep them from streaming out. The boy is disturbed. God knows, we recognize it now. He jiggles his leg again but says nothing. Movement out the window startles me but it's just the gulls leaving their boulder. One drops a clam onto the granite ledge and just leaves it there, smashed.

"Is she adopted?" he asks.

"No," I say. "She is from me and Carl. All the children are."

I hate myself for answering his questions because it's none of his business. But I think of his mother nursing him and holding his hand on the first day of school and worrying right now about where he is.

Do all mothers remember their children's first day at school? Carl took the day off from surgery. The hospital thought he'd lost his marbles, a well-respected surgeon with a long waiting list taking the day off to take his little girl to school. But he wanted to be there if she got scared and needed him.

We walked, Sylvie in the middle, the three blocks to the Milford Grammar School, chattering like magpies about snack time and recess and new kids and making paper chains. Sylvie's small hands gripped our fingers tight. She asked when it would be over, as if it were an operation.

I still remember her clothes. Red plaid jumper. White blouse, gray cardigan in case it got cold, black patent-leather Mary Janes, white ankle socks with Scottie dogs embroidered on them. Her braids were tied with red gros-grain ribbon and her part took a decided swerve along the back.

At the classroom door she turned and in her five-year-old voice told us to leave, that she was fine, although her face was smeared with tears and she had bitten a piece of loose skin from her lip so that it bled. She folded her arms in front of her and tapped her Mary Janes on the hard tile floor until we kissed the top of her head and walked down the corridor toward the door. Other parents cried, too. We weren't the only ones.

Did Jonah's parents cry when they left him at kinder-garten? Are his parents really dead? I wonder. He calms down, slows his jerking leg, sits back in the chair. His fin-gernails are clean, trimmed, his fingers smooth. Does some-one take care of him?

"Do you hear the loons?" he asks.

"They fly over to the pond," I say. "Every day we hear them."

"Young man, it's time for you to leave. Think about where you want to go. You can use the phone if you want."

"I'm waiting for someone."

"Are they coming to get you?"

"You might say that."

"When are they coming? What time?"

"Patience, Carl. Patience."

"No. You'll have to wait up at the road. Perhaps you should go to the police station."

"But my friend is coming here. To this house. Why would I go to the police?"

"I'll go and start the car," I say. "It takes a few minutes to warm up. Why don't you get your things together."

The telephone rings and Jonah jumps up to answer it.

"It's for me," he says to us. He turns away while he talks. I try not to listen. No, that's wrong. I try to listen but not make it obvious. I'm desperate to know who is on the other end of the phone. "I'm here," he says. "Yes. It's really me. Yes, I'm having a great chat. Where are you? I'll wait here, then. Yes, my beloved, I'll tell them."

"Tell who? Tell what?" Carl stands as he speaks. "Was that Sylvie?"

"No. I don't know Sylvie. She's much too old for me. My friend says to thank you for taking such good care of me," Jonah says. "But I need to stay here. I need to pave the way. You folks better pay attention. Got to straighten out a few things."

Why didn't I see how troubled he is? But I'm surprised that he really does have someone coming to pick him up and

I'm sorry for not believing him. When someone is clearly unbalanced, we tend to disbelieve everything they say. Is that fair?

Poor Sylvie. Once when I visited her in the mental hospital after the ill-fated graduation party, she told me her teacher had come to give her a diploma. She said she'd won the English prize. I patted her arm and told her that was lovely, how nice of him to come, and how smart she was to win the prize. When we got back to her room, there it was on the wall amid the spatters of God knows what. Sylvie had, in fact, won the thousand-dollar Arts and Letters Prize for her essay on ethics and the modern world, to be used at the university of her choice. And here she was in the mental hospital not "of her choice." Why hadn't I believed her when she told me? Would it have made a difference if I'd thrown my arms around her instead of patting her arm?

"It's warm today," I say. "There's shelter by the road. A big oak tree right where the driveway meets the highway. You can stand there and wait for your friend. You'll be fine."

"Go ahead, Jessie. Start the car and I'll drive him up to the highway."

Carl towers over Jonah. He's strong. Jonah walks toward the couch to get his jacket. Everything is fine.

"I'll only be a few minutes," I say. "Got to let the engine warm up." Carl sits down. I'm sure the boy is harmless but I plan on going with them up the drive.

# 9

## CARL

Jonah has changed since last night and I wonder if he's taking some kind of drug. I've seen him put something from his pocket into his mouth twice this morning. Once before Jessie came down and then again after breakfast. As crazy as Sylvie has been all these years, I've never been really afraid of her, but a sense of fear is gripping my gut at the moment. And I'm wondering who the "beloved" on the telephone might be. Probably not his mother, who's supposed to be dead. A girlfriend? A wife? A wrong number? Sylvie? I think that after I drop him off I'll call Galen at the town office to see if someone will check him out. God knows, the police have little enough to do around here.

While Jonah walks toward the couch to gather his belongings, I check the weather from the kitchen window. The thermometer reads almost sixty degrees and the clouds are high. He'll be fine. He seems like a smart boy. But then

Sylvie is smart, too. I'll be relieved when I get him to the highway. Then Jessie and I can get back to the business of finding our daughter.

"I'll only be a few minutes," Jessie says on the way to start the car. "Got to let the engine warm up."

Jessie looks like a girl this morning, as she has since I first met her. No makeup. No jewelry. And the most beautiful face I've ever seen. Her one long braid hangs halfway down her back the way it did when she was in college, and if it weren't gray, well . . . I love her old. I do.

I was at Harvard, just finishing up my medical studies. She was at Smith, preparing for her orals in history. We met in the Widener Library, where she was doing research. I followed her in through the front door although I had been on the way to lunch. I couldn't help myself. She wore an Indian skirt almost to her bare ankles, and a thick brown braid swung across her shoulder blades. Once, she glanced back to see who was trailing behind her. I stopped, pretended to study a notice on the wall, fell in again when she turned toward the history stacks. I lost her and began scurrying past the aisles of books, skimming down each one for the flash of red from the skirt. Finally I saw her, on the floor, her books strewn around her like dry leaves. She was crying. I loved her that soon. Before I even knew her.

"Almost ready?" I turn toward Jonah. "The car needs warming up. Jessie will be a few—"

"Hurry up. Over here. Sit down. I tried to get you to understand."

Jonah holds a small revolver pointed toward my head, a

roll of duct tape in his other hand. He rocks back and forth on his heels but keeps the gun steady. Is it my gun? It's my gun. Is it loaded? I can't remember. It's been in the cabinet drawer two years. No. I don't think it's loaded. But there were some new bullets on the top shelf behind the chafing dish. We bought the gun in case we found another wounded animal in the woods so we wouldn't have to kill it with a rock, like the deer with the fractured pelvis.

"What do you want?" I ask. "And what don't I understand?"

"That I need to be here. I have a mission. But now you want me to leave. You aren't what you seem, are you?"

"Is it money? Why don't you give me the gun."

"Why? Why? Because the gun is the force. You don't listen to me. I'm not big enough. But this is big enough, isn't it?" He waves the revolver now, toward the garage, toward the kitchen window, back to my head.

"I'll listen to you, son. What do you want?"

"Don't call me 'son.' I'm Jonah." His eyes aren't quite right. His tongue laps at the edges of his mouth. "Say it. 'Jonah.'"

"Are you really? Are you taking something? Some kind of drug?"

"Oh, you people are all about drugs, aren't you? You don't consider the power of God. Enough talk. You shut up and listen."

"I'm listening. But give me the gun. It's hard to listen with a gun pointed at you." I hear the engine running and hope Jessie stays in the car. Jessie couldn't take having a gun pointed at her. *Please, Jessie. Stay in the car until I can take care of this.*

"Sit down in that chair. Wrap this tape tight around your ankles. One ankle to each front chair leg. Do it. Now."

I walk toward him, my hand extended for the gun. "Please," I say as quietly as I can manage.

"Shut up. I don't want to shoot. You don't think I'll shoot, do you? Perhaps I'll shoot her instead."

Jessie with a hole in her? No. I can't take the chance. "No. You don't want to shoot anyone. I'll put on the tape."

"Come on. Wrap."

I sit in the heavy desk chair and begin to wrap. He paces around me and I try not to look at him. The ripping sound of the tape unrolling startles me. Is it always so loud? I spread my feet out a few inches before I join my ankles, in case I have to run, and hope he doesn't notice. I wrap it around one time and avoid overlapping.

"No. Undo the tape. I said ankles to chair legs. Separate them. Start over. Do it fast."

"Like this?"

"Once around?" he says. "Is once around enough? No. It isn't, is it, Carl? Wrap it around again."

He hasn't noticed the tape loose around my ankles. I wrap it around each ankle again, tugging it from its roll.

"Again."

The third time, he nods. I tear off the roll and slowly place it on the floor. I'm now attached to the damn chair. Jessie stamps her feet on the mat. It must be damp outside. *Please don't come in, Jessie.*

"Jessie," I say.

"Shut up, Carl," he says.

"Jessie, drive away. Go."

"What's that, Carl? Oh. Today's trash day. I'll put the can in the trunk." I hear her rattling around in the garage, rolling the trash can toward the car, hefting it into the trunk. She knows. She heard me. She's going to drive away and get the police. But then I hear her singing. She stamps her feet again. It's too late. "Oh, wait a minute. I'm missing the red skein." And she is gone.

"We don't have anything," I say. "Look. I can give you what we have. A hundred dollars. Maybe more."

"Shut up, old man. I don't want your money."

"What, then?"

I stand at the chair, my feet bound to the legs. The thing weighs a ton, a massive oak chair Jessie inherited from her grandfather.

"Sit," he says, as if I were a dog. "I said sit."

I don't move. I'm bigger than he is and he won't shoot me. "Is it your girlfriend who's coming?"

"Now you're the nosy one, Carl."

"She'll be upset if she sees this."

"Sees what? Me doing the right thing?"

"What do you want?"

Jessie opens the inside door and there we are. Me with my feet tied together with duct tape, and Jonah brandishing a revolver.

"You finish," he says. "Tape his arms to the chair because I have something to say."

"Carl? What's going on?"

"Do what he says."

"But that's your gun. It's never loaded."

"Oh, really?" Jonah aims through the kitchen window, at the osprey swooping over the clam flats, and fires. Jessie claps her hands over her ears. I follow the direction of the barrel. The bullet bored through the window without shattering it. Just a hole surrounded by small spokes like sunrays set in the glass. The osprey flies upward toward the clouds. Ducks flap on the opposite shore because of the noise. There are houses there. Someone will hear the shot. The gun is loaded. Could Hans and Marte hear the noise from their house? Someone will hear it and come to investigate. And then I remember that it's almost hunting season. Just about everyone around here is taking practice potshots at trees and tin cans and Frisbees.

I bought that gun for downed deer and mangled bears. Not for people. Not for human beings. I thought I should have one. You never know. There are five more possibilities in the cylinder. I sit down.

Jessie could have escaped through the door when Jonah fired the gun but she stands in the entryway like a schoolchild in a Christmas pageant. She makes no move to tape my arms to the chair nor to escape. She brings her braid to the front, strokes the end, allows herself to weep in silence in front of Jonah.

"Why didn't you listen to me?" Jonah asks.

"I . . . I should have," she says.

She needs me. That day years ago in the library at

Harvard, I picked her up from the floor, gathered her books, examined her bleeding elbow, pronounced her fit, and invited her for coffee. She wiped her eyes with the hem of that red print skirt, exposing her knees. Pretty knees with dimples, surprising for someone so slender, *n'est-ce pas?* I was into knees and I noticed things like that.

Today she wears blue jeans from yesterday; small spatters of paint dot her thighs. Her chin quivers. I know she tried not to cry. And if I weaken, she'll feel helpless. Jonah is only a few feet away. If I lurch toward him and grab the gun, we will be safe. But if I miss, Jessie may be hurt. Can I do it? Not with my ankles taped like this. I ache to kiss her eyes, make her tea, but I mouth words about escaping when he turns his back to confront her. She doesn't see me. She's gazing at Jonah now through tears. I work my feet back and forth, trying to free myself from the tape. If I bend to unfasten it, I know he'll hear the ripping of the tape. I mouth, "Ask him for the gun," over and over. Perhaps he'll give it to her, a mother, a woman.

"May I have it?" she asks. I can hardly hear her, and her arms don't stretch out to receive it. "The gun."

Jonah lowers his head as if he is considering her suggestion. Jessie pays no attention to my charades about escape. She walks slowly toward him, her hand now extended. He taps on the floor with his sneaker. I rise again from my chair without making a sound but he hears me. I think it's because Jessie glanced in my direction.

"Sit down," Jonah says. Jonah brings in a kitchen chair and sits down as if the command was to himself, but when

I don't move to sit, he waves the gun at me again. "Please. I am here to pave the way. You do exactly what I tell you to do. I have God behind me." From his pocket he takes something—another pill, I think—which he shoves into his mouth and swallows without water. "Now. Lady. Please tape Carl's arms to the chair."

"I'll listen to you," Jessie says. "Please. Don't hurt us."

The telephone begins to ring. When I got up this morning, I turned off the answering machine because I knew we'd be right here. For a moment it appears that Jonah will answer, but he ignores it. When Jessie starts toward the ringing phone, Jonah jerks the gun to point it at her, and she backs away. Twelve, thirteen. The ringing finally stops.

"What if it's your girlfriend?" I say, wishing I'd thought of that when it began. "Maybe she's delayed. Maybe she isn't coming."

"Shut up, Carl," he says. "Why are you doing this? Don't you love me?"

"Love you? I don't even know you."

"But I know you. I know you, Carl. Yes sirree, I know you well. I know who you really are."

"Know me? How? Who are you? I think I know who you are. You have to leave."

"Oh, no, I don't."

Once when Charlie was a small boy, he looked like this boy, defiant, scared, a lock of hair flopping on his forehead.

"Oh, yes, I am," he'd said when I told him he couldn't go ice fishing with the older boys without an adult. When he pulled his snow pants up and shoved his feet into his boots,

I made no attempt to stop him. I tied his hat under his chin while he put on his mittens.

"Will you make me a sandwich?" he had asked.

"Sure, Son. Peanut butter?"

"Dad, do you like fish? I'll bring you one home."

"Charlie, I've told you that you can't go ice fishing alone. You aren't allowed. It's too dangerous. But of course you know that, don't you?"

"Just pretend, Dad," he said. "Not real ice fishing. Just pretend. In the backyard. I'll bring you and Mom a pretend fish."

It terrified me to think he could fall through the ice into frigid water without me there to save him. I still remember the sense of relief I felt that day when I knew he wouldn't go without permission.

I think this boy could shoot me. Even worse, I think he could shoot my Jess. Perhaps, like my Charlie, he'll change his mind. He'll put the gun down and leave.

It's been a very long time since a gun has been pointed at me. I never thought it would happen again, certainly not in America, land of the free. Back then, guns sounded day and night, indiscriminate shots at anything that moved. Once, a new guard practiced by shooting at my feet while I danced. He wanted me to waltz around the courtyard while he tried to aim as close as possible without hitting me. I was naked and the cold stiffened my joints until I could barely lift my feet from the frozen mud. My family stood in silent columns with the others. I watched my mother try to look beyond me so she couldn't see my feeble attempts at dance and view my exposed sex. But she saw. I know she saw. When the guard grazed my small toe with one of his bullets, he tossed me a violin and made me play while my uncle danced. My uncle's genitals were shot off. We weren't allowed to help him, of course. He froze during the night and I was conscripted into the camp orchestra to take his place. That violin saved my life.

But all that is in the past, left in Europe. Now I live in the United States, where people don't shoot other people and make them do things that have no dignity.

"Tape him. Hurry up."

When Jessie hesitates, Jonah holds his arm out straight toward her, the barrel of the revolver close to her heart. She pulls the duct tape off the roll and stretches it over the arm of my sweatshirt.

"No. Pull the shirt up. I want to see the fish. Pull it up. Stick the tape to his skin. Leave the fish showing. There you go. That's right." He doesn't notice that I lift up my arm to keep the tape loose. "I was reborn in the belly of a fish, you know. Given another chance, you might say. That makes us relatives, doesn't it?"

# 10

## JESSIE

WHAT IF JONAH shoots me in the heart? How will it feel, I wonder, to have a bullet pierce my chest, crack a rib, blow a hole in my left ventricle? Will I really feel anything or will it be over too soon for any awareness? While I'm wrapping the tape around Carl's bare arm, Jonah will have to shoot me through my back. Perhaps it won't hurt quite as much if I don't see it coming.

If I wrap the tape an inch at a time, press it down onto Carl's flesh, I can prolong my time with him. What does this Jonah want, anyway? Is he just crazy and did he fall upon our house by mistake? That couldn't be. The smell of the duct tape adhesive makes me woozy. If I keel over, will he shoot me? I think Carl is raising his arm to keep the tape loose. He's going to escape. I know it. We're going to get out of this.

And what about Jonah? He says we're relatives because

of the fish. Is that just crazy talk or do we have some connection? Does he know our daughter? Yes. That's who he is. It must be.

The only sounds in the house are the quiet humming of the refrigerator and the car engine and the jerk of the duct tape each time I tug on it. I don't know what he's doing behind me but I sense the muzzle of the revolver pointed through my spine. Carl isn't looking at me. He watches his own shoes. I press lightly on the tape so that it catches only the hairs on his arms, little by little across his wrists. When I kiss the top of his head, he shudders. Fear? Embarrassment? I don't know. Both, perhaps. I run my index finger down his sad cheek to the corner of his mouth. His tongue touches the tip. I allow my finger to enter his mouth, just to the joint. He closes his lips around it. I whisper love words to him and he nods just enough for me to feel his head move. There is no sound from behind me.

The first time he took my finger into his mouth, sucked gently as a sleeping baby would, we made love in a cemetery near my school. We huddled in the shadows behind a large stone while we undressed. That was the first time I felt the scars on his back.

"Don't," he said when I slid my hand along his back. Squares of hard raised flesh. "Don't. It's from the war."

When I'm finished with the tape, I turn away from Carl. Jonah still sits in the chair, watching us, weeping to himself now. The gun points toward the floor. It has begun to rain, and fog obscures my rock through the window.

"He loves you," Jonah says.

"Yes," I say.

"Someone loves me, too."

"Yes, Jonah. I'm sure they do."

He wipes his face with the sleeve of his shirt. The gun stays pointed down.

"Jess," Carl says. I can barely hear him. "The gun."

I walk toward Jonah. He looks weak, frail, frightened. "Everything will be all right." I open my arms toward him because he is like a child. Like my child. "Let me take the gun from you. It is bad."

"Sit down," he says. "On the couch." He gestures with the gun again and I back up until I feel the cushions at the backs of my legs. I lower myself until I perch on the edge.

"What do you want?" I ask.

"I want love, too," he says.

"But you said someone loves you."

"Yes. They're coming here."

"Coming here? But what do you want from us? We don't even know you."

"Get out," Carl says. "Leave us alone."

"Oh, my, Carl. Don't be so angry. If you're angry with me, you're angry with God."

"Do you want something to eat, Jonah?" I ask.

"Lunch. Is it time for lunch?"

"I'll make something."

"Bring it in here. If you do anything bad, I'll shoot Mr. Carl here."

On the way to the kitchen, I pass within a foot of Jonah. I am frightened, but something makes me want to touch his shoulder. How could I feel that way? And why the hell did we ever get the damn gun? I consider grabbing it from him as I pass, but at the last moment he shifts in the chair and aims at Carl.

I make Swiss cheese sandwiches with mustard, cut them in triangles, scatter them on a platter. Jonah places another video into the machine and turns it on with the remote. It's *Planet of the Apes*. When can I act? My mind scurries for ideas. Carl is no help. When Jonah's back is to me, I consider throwing a knife at him, but I envision it bouncing off his shoulder and clattering to the floor. And then he will be angry and he'll hurt someone. Perhaps Carl will make a commotion and I can throw a rock from the windowsill. I slip one into my pocket, a jagged chunk of granite the size of an egg. I found it on the shore and brought it home because it was pink with streaks of red and black through it. I thought it was pretty.

Jonah jerks the video out of the machine and shoves in another. I rustle through the refrigerator, searching for time to think. If I threw the pound of butter at him, it might knock him off balance enough for me to hit him with the rock. And then I picture him as a child and wonder if I have the guts to hurt him. Could I crack his skull with my rock? And would he really shoot us? I find some celery in the vegetable crisper, take it out, cut it into small sticks, strew them over the cheese sandwiches. How about tea? It would be hot. Scalding. I run water into the kettle.

"No tea," he says. "No coffee. Nothing hot."

I fill three water glasses from the pitcher. Glass. That's

it. Broken glass at his throat. But I won't be able to cut him. The blood.

He throws the video from the machine against the wall and digs around on the shelf for another. He motions for me to place the lunch tray on the small side table near the couch.

"Give him some," he says.

I've never fed Carl before. He fed me once. A spoonful of fish chowder. After I had Sylvie. But this is a first. He chews at the end of the cheese sandwich until it's half gone. Crumbs drop onto his lap. I take a bite from his end. That's all we eat. Carl says he isn't hungry. I'm hungry but I say I'm not.

Jonah eats all the rest. When he finishes, he reaches for another video. He's been through the beginnings of most movies on the shelf. The last one is our family. Years of home movies and photos recorded onto a two-hour video. Charlie gave it to us for Christmas the year he got married, and we watch it on each of the children's birthdays. Most of it is Sylvie because she was the first born, and the first child always has more pictures taken. The music was added by the video people. I hate it. It sounds like elevator music and we always turn the sound off when we watch it. But Jonah has the sound on. Not loud. But audible.

"I have to go to the bathroom," Carl says.

Jonah clicks a button on the remote and the screen turns blue. Clicks another one and the blue flickers and dies. The horrid music stops. "Does Mr. Carl need a bath? Is he getting ready?" He turns toward Carl with the gun, waits for an answer to the ridiculous question.

Carl slumps with his ankles and arms taped to the heavy chair, like a man living out his final moment in Old Sparky, waiting for the jolt to end everything. But he's thinking. As soon as he's free, we'll act. Carl's going to save us.

"Well, Carl? A nice warm bath?"

"I need to urinate," Carl says.

"Oh, well then, let's find something for you to piss into."

"I'll come right back. Please. I need to go into the bathroom."

"The missus will find you something. Get him a bottle or a jar or a bucket. The water pitcher. Get it."

"Let Jessie cut the tape. I'll just be a minute. I promise I'll come back."

"No one can escape from God."

"That's right. See? I can't escape."

"No, you can't. I'm not going to let you. You're not ready yet, Carl. No. Not ready. You haven't changed your life. You still need help."

"Jessie," Carl says, "get the scissors from the hook. Cut the tape."

"My mission is more important than your pathetic life. Don't move, missus."

"I'll stay here with you," I say. "That way Carl won't try to escape. You see?"

"Shut up. Both of you." He stands, digs into his pocket for another of those pills he's taking. "You. Get something for him to piss in."

I find I'm getting used to having a gun pointed at me. I've had nightmares about that kind of thing but now I look right at it and follow the track the bullet might take if he fires. Into the front door. Past the floor lamp. Through the center of the television screen. Into my brain.

"Go on. I don't want to shoot anyone, but if God says, 'Do it,' then I do it. Get the thing."

When he waves the gun at Carl, I'm not used to it anymore. Funny. I can stand it pointed at me but not at Carl. "Yes. I'll get it."

All the way over to the counter I imagine Carl's humiliation. First I feed him. Then I hold a container for him to pee into. Carl's a private person. He doesn't even pee in front of the boys. He always shuts the door when they're home. Says he has a shy bladder. But I'll pee in front of anyone. That's one of our differences.

The pitcher is plenty big enough. I empty the lunch water into the sink and consider smashing the thing on the edge of the counter. Then I'd have a smooth handle with a jagged glass weapon attached. But he might shoot Carl. I touch the rock in my pocket. Perhaps that's the thing to use.

"Could you turn away?" I ask Jonah.

"What's the matter? Modest?"

"Yes," Carl says.

"I'm responsible for you two. Now. Do it. Unzip him."

Again my back is in the trajectory of the barrel of the gun, but I hear Jonah walking toward us while I lower the pitcher to the floor. Does Carl undo his belt when he urinates? I can't honestly remember. I fumble with the zipper of his fly. I think Carl cries inside of himself, because I can feel his belly trembling.

The boy stands beside me as if he is going to help. Perhaps it would be better if Carl just let it go. Wet into the chair. I look at him. His eyes are away from me, toward the front door. I want to catch his attention because of the glass pitcher. There isn't anything nearby to smash it on. The chair is wood; the floor is wood as well. Not hard enough to break the glass. Jonah shuffles beside me, sniffs, clears his throat. If I reached out I could touch his leg. He's too close. I can sense his breath, the warmth of it, the taste of Swiss cheese and mustard. My fingers can't seem to maneuver the zipper. I slide the end of his belt through the first part of the buckle, pull it back, and release it from the metal pin. Carl sighs as I open the belt, glad of the release.

"Hurry up."

Jonah walks around behind me to the other side. Carl turns his head away toward the kitchen, toward the bullet hole in the window.

"I don't have to go anymore," Carl says.

"Shut up, Carl. You don't know what you want. Pull his thing out. Hurry up. We don't have all day."

"But we do have all day," I say.

Jonah hits me. Not hard. But it's the first time anyone's hit me since I was a child. Just flips the back of his hand on my head. It hurts and the tears come, although I will myself to hold them back.

"Stop it," Carl says. "It's not too late to just walk out that door. We won't tell anyone about this."

"Carl, I have to do this. God is watching me."

"God? You think God wants you to hurt people?"

"If I have to, Carl. If I have to. Now. Get to it. Finish what you started, little lady."

"Oh, God," Carl says. "Lord in heaven."

"You praying, Carl? That's good. That'll help. And you. You want another bop on the head?"

"No. I'll do it. But please, step away."

He doesn't, but with both hands I fiddle with the button on Carl's pants until it slides through the hole. Carl shifts in the chair to make it easier to pull the zipper down. He nods when I hesitate at the next step. First I pick up the empty water pitcher, balance it on his thighs. Only then do I spread the opening in his boxer shorts. He is large. Not sex large. Just large, which makes it difficult to bring it out. He opens his legs for me to place the pitcher there, in the space in front of him. I lay his flesh on the smooth glass and hover my palm over it to keep Jonah from seeing.

Carl's hand tries to reach as if to help me. "It's all right, Carl," I say. "Just relax."

"Please, turn away," he says to me. And we wait.

I stare at the floor next to his chair. Jonah makes no attempt to move, continues to gaze at the water pitcher. Carl begins. The liquid flows into the pitcher, warming the glass. Carl sobs once, heaving his shoulders forward. He continues. The pitcher is half full. There'll be no escape in the bathroom. The bathroom. Yes. I can smash the pitcher on the sink. Or the toilet. Jonah will come to see what happened. I'll hit him with the glass. Cut him. Then take the gun.

When Carl is finished, I tuck him back into his boxers

before I remove the pitcher to the floor. I buckle the belt just enough to keep the pants from falling when he gets up. The rest I leave unfastened.

"Not circumcised, eh, Carl? Now why doesn't that surprise me? Did I expect a circumcised dick? You're a Frenchman, or are you a German? Why should you be cut? You're not a Jew, are you? You're not one of God's chosen. Why, then, Carl? Why, then, the fish?"

# 11

## JESSIE

THE ATMOSPHERE IN OUR small house congeals around us. Sounds and movements feel slow, loud, sloggy. Carl sinks into the chair as if he were part of the upholstery and has ceased to be Carl. Of course Carl must be part Jewish. Why else the tattoo? His family wasn't religious. That's why he isn't circumcised. His father was French. And they never went to synagogue. It didn't matter to the Nazis. It wasn't about the religion, anyway. It was about the blood.

Should I answer Jonah's questions? Carl never talked about his past, and no wonder. It was a terrible time in the history of the world. Why talk about it? I tried once or twice to ask questions myself but I felt I was prying into something very private. It was our only secret. I told Carl almost everything about myself. Even things that I never told another soul. And he told me everything except for the part about the war. Just that one time when he had too much wine and he told about running away and his family's getting shot behind him. That's all. And the violin. He doesn't talk about that at all.

Sylvie once asked questions about his back and his tattoo, and Carl took her on his lap and said that some very bad men did reprehensible acts to other human beings in the name of medicine and that things like that don't happen in this day and age and in this country. But sometimes I wonder where the United States was when this was all going on. I know we fought in the war, but did we do enough? I've heard stories of boatloads of Jews being turned away and sent back to certain death. Did that happen?

Carl always wears a long-sleeved shirt, so the issue doesn't come up often. But I suppose it always hovers, back there, somewhere. I think Sylvie told her brothers and said to leave that subject alone. And now this boy, Jonah, with a gun in his hand, asks impossible questions that are none of his business. How dare he.

The pitcher is heavier than I expect and I cradle it in both hands to avoid sloshing urine onto the floor. At each step I expect Jonah to stop me, tell me to leave the pitcher on the table or on the floor, but there's no sound from behind me. The downstairs bathroom is small because we rarely use it, although it does have a shower. One of those freestanding, ready-made ones with a cloth curtain. When we have grandchildren it will be handy to rinse off salt and sand and beach debris.

I push the door mostly closed so that he can't see me from the room and I pee as noisily as I can. He won't dare try to come in here while I am doing something as personal as that. I know the sound of the flush won't obliterate the sound of smashing glass, but perhaps it'll muddy it up. This has to be done right. I may have only one chance.

I straighten myself up and poise the pitcher over the toilet, pour, and rinse it out in the sink. Then I push the handle down until the rush of water begins. Now. I bring the glass pitcher down hard on the edge of the white porcelain sink, and pieces fly in every direction until I am left holding the glass handle studded with jagged shards. I don't hear any steps stamping toward the bathroom. Perhaps he didn't hear the breaking glass. I move the weapon around to my back. I hear the thwack first. Then Carl's groan. The door slams into the table when I kick it open. He's hit Carl. Jonah has belted Carl with the gun. Carl's head hangs into his lap but I see the blood dripping onto his pants.

"Carl?"

"Shut up. That was one stupid move."

"I've broken the pitcher. It just fell."

Jonah begins to dance toward me, kind of a little skipping dance, the dance of a child. He sings in a small, high voice, a singsongy falsetto. "You're not going to hurt me, you're not going to—"

"I'll clean it up," I say.

"What's hiding behind your back?"

"Please leave us alone," Carl says.

"What, Carl? I can't hear you. You're whispering. How do you expect God to know what's going on if you don't speak up?"

Carl turns his face toward us until I see where the blood is coming from. His front tooth is missing. It's in his lap, gleaming white surrounded by drips of blood.

"Carl? Do you have something to say? Come on. Out with it. Cat got your tongue?"

I take a tentative step forward. Jonah's only three paces away, at most. Behind my back I grip the cool glass tight.

"Carl thinks you should leave us alone," I say. "Do you think God would like what you are doing? What kind of a God do you know?"

"My God is my business. Now. What're you hiding there?"

"Hiding?" I transfer the pitcher from one hand to the other behind me and show him my empty hands, just like a child doing a simple magic trick for her first audience. Why doesn't he see the flash of broken glass, notice my ludicrous sleight of hand?

"Look, lady, mother of Sylvie, you try anything funny, and his wrinkly old dick's coming off. You get that?"

"Yes. I've got it." I lean against the wall near the kitchen, attempt to conceal my glass weapon. He seems to have forgotten about the pitcher's breaking in the bathroom. He saunters over to the sink and pours himself a glass of water, waving the gun all the while. I think he takes several of the small white pills from his pocket and swallows them with the water.

"Time for a little entertainment," he says. He swipes the arm of his shirt across his wet mouth. "I never finished the story of Sylvie."

Jonah presses the on button for the VCR and settles into the soft chair beside Carl. The only sign of nervousness is his constantly jiggling leg. Sylvie's dressed in organdy and patent leather. She's ten or eleven. Darling. The horrible canned music pounds out "Raindrops Keep Fallin' on My Head" while Sylvie practices her steps for her tap-dance recital, completely out of sync with the "raindrops." What if I ask him to lower the sound? He might get angry and I'll lose my chance. I take another step toward him and he doesn't notice. I could throw the broken pitcher at him. But what if it misses? I'll take one more step.

The telephone rings. He watches me to see if I'll answer it. If I do, he'll see my weapon. I wait for it to ring again before I move toward it.

"Oh, no. I'll answer that," he says. He flicks off the video just as Sylvie takes her curtsy. Her red bow is crooked. Funny. I never noticed that before.

"Hello?" he says. "Sylvie?" Does he think she is calling? Is she calling? "Oh, sorry. They've stepped out. May I take a message?"

He's preoccupied. Now I could hit him with the pitcher. One step toward him. And another. He's listening to the caller. I swing my arm around, my weapon sparkling in the sunlight, swiping the air just inches from Jonah's shoulder. He sees it, ducks, aims the gun at Carl.

"Oh, I see. Well, I know they're very concerned about their daughter. I'd be glad to give them a message." He waves the gun around, leveling the trajectory directly into Carl's mouth, which is hanging open and drooling blood onto his arm. "I'm a close family friend, you know. I know all about the problem with Sylvie." Jonah listens for a moment longer, then drops the receiver into the cradle without another word.

"Did they say anything? Is there any news?"

"You fucking bitch," he says. "I ought to kill you."

"You can't kill me, Jonah. I'm Sylvie's mother. She'd never forgive you."

"But I can kill Mr. Carl, here. He's a fake and a liar."

"No, Jonah. Sylvie wouldn't like that, either."

"You're trying to control me. Why are you doing that? Where is she? You're her mother. Don't you know where she is?"

"No. I don't."

"We wait, then. You and me and Mr. Carl."

"What do you want from us?"

"Give me that. Pass it slow. No funny stuff or I shoot the balls off the old man."

I almost saved us. Almost saving is like being a little pregnant or coming in second. As he takes the handle of the pitcher from me, our hands brush against each other. He's touched her with those hands. I know it. He's touched my Sylvie in intimate ways. There has to be some good in there.

"Jonah, you know Sylvie, don't you? You know our daughter. You didn't have your gear stolen."

"You know where she is," he says, "don't you?"

"Maybe in the tree," I say. "In the pine. Did she tell you about the pine?"

"Yes. She did. The pine tree."

"Yes. You should go and see if she's there. We'll wait right here for you."

"You think I'm crazy, don't you? I want to tell you about why I'm here. You. Go over by Carl. That's right. Sit down next to him."

I lift Carl's tooth from his thigh and tuck it into a wad of tissue from my pocket. I leave it on the side table because I always save teeth that come out. The tooth fairy comes and I tuck the teeth away in my top bureau drawer. I still have all the children's teeth in a tin box next to my socks.

Then I pat the blood spatters dry. His fingers curl upward as if they belong to someone dead, and they lie still like sausages when I wipe the blood from them. He thanks me.

"She promised she'd meet me here. She gave me directions. Are you both comfortable?"

"No," I say. "Not comfortable."

"She loves me," he says.

"Yes, I'm sure she does."

"Want to know why I left?"

"Tell me," I say.

Carl says nothing. Our arms touch lightly, enough for me to feel his distress. I press my arm onto his.

"Look," Jonah says, "I don't have to tell you anything. This is between me and God. Have you got a cookie? Something to munch on?"

"In the cupboard," I say. "Second door."

For a moment he turns his back on us but I no longer have my weapon and I'm not sure I can find the strength to hit him with the rock from my pocket. It isn't very large and my hands aren't as strong as they used to be.

"Carl? Are you in pain?"

"Not much," he says. "Jess. I'm sorry. I lied to you."

"Don't worry about that now," I say. "What did you lie about?"

"About my family. About the camp. There are reasons."

"You two having a chat?" Jonah asks. He passes me the box of gingersnaps after he scoops out a handful. I shake my head. I don't want a cookie. "Now then, where were we?"

"You were telling me why you left. Why you came here."

He sits down in the chair, legs spread out in front of him, cookies in his lap. He holds the pistol pointed at us. When I motion with my hand to please lower it, he does.

"I have a very intimate relationship with God," he says. "There are only a few of us, you know."

He bites off half a cookie before he continues. In a strange way, I feel as if we're sitting around chatting and snacking but we are the guests and he is the host. He appears relaxed, offers me another cookie, and looks disappointed when I refuse. Carl doesn't respond at all.

"Only a hundred of us, to be exact," Jonah says. "He speaks to me just like a person would. He says, 'Jonah, today you will pray for one hour,' or 'Go to Sylvie's parents and prepare them.'"

"Prepare us for what?" Carl asks. I'm startled when he speaks. His words are mushy because of the missing tooth and the pain I know he has in his face.

"Well, now. Can't you tell what I'm preparing you for?"

Jonah rubs his chin. The sound is raspy because he hasn't shaved in several days. He wipes the corners of his mouth. I don't think he has any idea what he's supposed to prepare us for.

"Are you asking us to repent?" I ask. "To save ourselves, like the people of Nineveh? Isn't that what Jonah does?"

"I love her," he says. His voice is so low I barely hear his words. "Where is she?"

"Maybe she's in the tree. Wouldn't you like to go and find out?"

"She's going to meet me here. She promised. I'm here to get things ready." The hand holding the gun hangs limply at his side, the muzzle almost touching the floor. He eats one last cookie. "How far is the tree?"

"Not far. Maybe ten minutes' walk. What do you think Sylvie would do if she saw you with the gun pointed at us? Don't you think she'd be upset?"

The gun clatters to the floor before he can answer, and I'm on my feet, running toward him, the granite in my hand. I'll strike him on the temple. He will fall. I will shoot him. No. Yes. Behind me Carl whispers, "Be careful, be careful." Before I can raise my arm against him, Jonah scoops up the gun from the floor and shoves it onto my throat, pushes me back.

"Going to hit me with that rock?"

"Jonah, we're trying to save ourselves. We're helping you. I don't think you're doing the right thing." The cold metal hums with my words, distorts my voice, pushes into my larynx. His finger is too close to see clearly. Is it on the trigger?

# 12

## CARL

"BE CAREFUL," I say. "Be careful."

I'm not sure she hears me. I say it again but barely have time to finish. He shoves that goddamn gun against her neck, pushing her, pushing her. She grips the chunk of granite in her hand. She speaks with a new sense of authority, my Jess, directly to a man who has the live end of a revolver shoved against her throat. The rock clatters to the floor beside her when he tells her to drop it. She's like a dog being reprimanded for chewing a forbidden toy, like Reba when she stole Jessie's undies and my socks from the laundry.

Jessie doesn't back away from the pistol. What has happened in one day? Jessie, who hates guns. Jessie, who pleaded with me not to buy it. Now she stands firm. Will Jonah shoot her? Will he shoot anyone? He's taken a handful of those little white pills. He could do anything, I suspect.

"Come on, you two," Jonah says, still holding the gun at her. "You're making it hard for me. Sylvie's waiting for me to prepare the way. This is all for her. Don't you see?"

It's hard to believe he is a madman, a criminal, a miscreant. What if Jess is shot? What if he pulls the trigger and she falls with a thud onto the floor beside the granite? Then my arms will rip the goddamn duct tape and squeeze his throat until the breath goes out of him. But if I can do it after she's dead, why can't I do it now? I struggle with my arms and legs against the tape but there's little movement except for a quiet thump of the chair.

"Please," Jonah says. "I don't want to shoot anyone, but I will if I have to. Just do as I say."

"Well," Jessie says, "what *do* you say, Jonah of God?"

Jonah releases Jessie and begins pacing, waving the gun. He wipes at his chin as if there were food stuck there. I think Jessie's strength scares the bejesus out of him. Sweat beads on his forehead, making his bangs damp. He stops pacing and turns to face her.

"I have to know you. Be important in your eyes."

"You are important."

"I don't feel it. That's why I need this. I don't feel that you respect me."

"Oh, yes," she says. "We definitely do, don't we, Carl?"

I can't find the strength to speak. I nod slowly but no words come and it isn't convincing enough.

"It's Sylvie's idea. She said to listen to my voices, that it was God speaking. He said to get you ready for us. And to cleanse Carl."

"Cleanse from what?" I ask.

"Shut up," Jonah says. "You're trying to trick me, divert me from my mission. I know. I decide what to cleanse."

He seems to have forgotten about Jessie and is focusing on me now. His arm absently lowers the gun toward me. I command my mouth to spit razors at him but nothing forms under my tongue. The hole where my tooth used to be throbs. How stupid I am. I can't move. I can't help my wife. I can't even piss by myself.

"The police will find you," I say.

Jonah considers what I said. He licks the corners of his mouth, and his eyes focus up at the ceiling as if he's waiting for an idea.

"Look, Mr. Carl, you do what I say and I won't hurt you. I promise. But you have to do what I say. Art. The way to intimacy is through art."

Jonah finds his idea. But what in God's name could he be looking for in the drawer? Paints? And paper? Charcoal pencils? He pulls a small penknife from his jacket pocket and sharpens one of the pencils. He whittles the tip, allowing the shavings to scatter on the floor. He juggles the gun and pencil in one hand and the knife in the other. How can he do that? I wait for him to put the gun down on the table, but he doesn't. Then he loads his free arm with the art supplies, still gripping the handle of the gun tight in his hand.

"What are you doing?" Jessie asks.

"Getting to know you better," he says. "Relax. Pretend we're meeting for the first time. I want to see what Mr. Carl here can do with this stuff."

"Not much with my hands tied," I say.

"Cut that tape," Jonah says. "Slowly so I can see every-thing."

He signals with his eyes toward a pair of scissors hanging on a nail in the beam that separates the kitchen from the living room. Jessie moves with the grace of a ballet dancer toward the scissors, and I close my eyes and pray that she doesn't come at him with the sharp points, that she does as he asks. Jonah shadows her over to the scissors and back to my chair, hovers while she snips at the gray tape a bit at a time until it's severed through on both sides. She leaves the tape stuck across my arms. I think she doesn't want to yank it off and pull my hairs with it. I think she doesn't want to hurt me. Jonah tells her to return the scissors to the nail. She watches him all the way to see if he is paying attention, to see if she might have a chance to slip something sharp into her pocket. But he watches her closely and she hooks one of the scissor holes over a nail, and the blades fall open along the wooden beam.

My hands and wrists are stiff from being taped to the chair. They seem foreign to me, as if they belong to another man, a large old man, a useless, doddering fool. When I try to make a fist, my hand seems bloated, puffy, like rising bread, good only for resting on the arm of a chair. I close my eyes and I imagine my punch, the hardest I can muster, spreading blandly across Jonah's craggy chin, soft, flaccid, futile.

"Paint," he says. "Draw something personal. The way to intimacy is through artistic expression. Don't you know that, Carl? You heard that before?"

"No. I haven't." I look at Jonah, who is holding out a sketch pad. I almost laugh out loud. Here we are, being tortured by a madman, and I'm going to draw a seagull in the midst of it all.

"That's what Sylvie said. 'Get to know them. They're family.' So that's what I'm doing. Getting to know you. Now, draw something."

"What?"

"If I tell you, it isn't personal anymore. I don't know you, Carl. I don't know what you think about."

The scene through the kitchen window is far enough away to resemble a framed sketch. When I finish drawing, my fingers will be loosened up, ready to hit him. I clasp the sketch pad from his outstretched hand and lay it on my lap. He plucks the sharpened pencil from his shirt pocket and waves it under my nose until I take it. Our fingers touch. If I could be sure of my strength, I would turn his wrist until the bones snapped, but I'm afraid. Instead I draw a horizon line across the paper.

Jonah steps back just a little so that he's beyond my reach. Jessie is thinking. She glances around for weapons, for ways to escape, for a break in his concentration. I begin to draw the boulder bulging from the rocky shore, round and prominent, replacing some of the horizon line. Wisps of sea grass, small round stones smoothed by centuries of water, strokes of the sharpened pencil. Blurry marks made with the side of the charcoal. I'm a decent artist. Bushes and clumps of seaweed emerge from the paper. Waves, whitecaps on the water. The point of land projects from the right.

The edge of our picnic table pokes into the lower corner. He peeks over the paper, my gun gripped in his hand, pointing toward my wife. My hands seem feeble. The pencil falls onto the charcoal boulder.

"That's it?" he asks. "Finished?"

I need more time. I pick up the pencil and search the scene. The gulls have gone but I draw twelve thin, paired lines from the boulder toward the sky, twelve reedy legs, six gulls in silhouette because it's too complicated to draw them facing us. Is it almost suppertime? I draw the gulls in groups. Two and four.

"I don't see any gulls," Jonah says. "That's good, Carl. You love birds, don't you, Carl?"

I almost expect Jessie to ask why the gulls face the sun, but there is silence in the house except for the barely discernible car engine outside and the scuff of my pencil across the smooth paper. I fill in details. Seams of dark granite across the boulder. The birch stump that looks like a dragon, a day sailer with the jib billowing, mounds of rockweed heaped by the tide onto the pebble shore. All I see now is the drawing framed by the window, a tranquil scene, the world of wild things in harmony with one another.

"That's enough," he says.

"I'm almost finished."

"You're finished with that one," he says. "Draw something else." He rips the seashore scene from the notebook and passes it to Jessie.

"What else?"

"Carl, why don't you draw Sylvie's tree?" Jessie's voice is strong. She has an idea.

"Yes. I'll draw Sylvie's tree," I say. *What*, I ask myself, *is she thinking?* But there's no time to speculate. Jonah slaps his hand across my notebook, leaving his palm on the place where I want to draw the tree.

"No tree. Draw something else." He removes his hand and steps back.

I begin to draw the kitchen table, the candles, the tea-cups, two of the ladder-back chairs pulled up to the edge of the pine tabletop.

"No," he says. When he rips the sheet from the pad, the edge of the paper cuts the back of my hand and a drop of blood seeps through. I wait for it to drip down onto the pa-per, flow onto the smooth white surface, but it beads at the wound and settles back down into itself.

"Draw her," he says.

"Jessie?"

"That's personal, isn't it, Carl?"

"I don't want to. I don't want to draw her."

"You don't seem to understand. Sylvie wants me to know you."

"Put the gun down, Jonah," Jessie says. "We'll tell you all about ourselves, won't we, Carl?"

"Yes. We will."

"Art," he says. "It's through art. That's how the truth comes."

"I was born near Paris in nineteen thirty—"

"Shut up, Carl. I don't mean that kind of garbage. I mean, who are you, Carl? Draw. Draw your wife."

He jabs her in the ribs with his index finger. It hurts. I can tell. She slumps to the side, holds herself. I pick up the blasted pencil again. He wants me to draw my wife? I'll draw my wife. I make a soft line down the middle of the paper, her center. I'll draw her upright, happy, strong. Jonah steps back to give us room and sits in the chair by the art chest.

Jessie stands up straight, sets her shoulders square. Her braid flips over her shoulder and she strokes the loose end while I draw her arms. We try to talk with our eyes. Her mouth twists toward the back door, her glance following. Jonah can't see her face. I work quickly so he won't interrupt. I draw the paint-spattered blue jeans that hug her bottom, her sneakers, the knobby fingers that fondle her hair. It's the best I've done of Jessie. Her wrinkled eyelids surround perfect young eyes, and her chin sags only a little. Her mouth is so Jessie, but so Sylvie, too. They look alike, *n'est-ce pas?*

"Hold it up so I can see," Jonah says.

I obey. He glances from the drawing to the model, back and forth, following with the gun, the blasted gun. How could I have been so stupid as to buy a gun? Jonah's expression is obscure. How could he not like it? It's Jessie.

"Take them off," he says. He's looking at Jessie. She turns toward him, flings her braid to the back. "Take them off. Everything."

"What?" she asks. I can barely hear her hushed voice. "What did you say?"

"Your clothes. Off."

"My clothes? All my clothes?"

"You heard me," he says. "Glasses, too. Just drop—" The telephone saves everything.

"Hello?" Jonah says. He sounds like a normal man answering a normal telephone call. "Oh, I'm terribly sorry. They've gone out again. But they said to take a message. I'm a close family friend. Have you heard anything from the poor woman?" Jonah walks with the telephone, back and forth. Should I call out? Should I scream? But the bullets. I'm afraid of the bullets. "Sylvie's such a dear. Isn't it too bad." Jonah clicks with his tongue. I think they're talking to him. He holds the telephone out and I hear a voice but I can't make out the words. Jonah smiles and says, "Goodbye," before he replaces the telephone in its cradle. It's too late to shout.

"Come on then, Sylvie's mother. Glasses first. Just begin. Pull that sweater over your head. Don't you know how to undress?"

Jessie doesn't move. She's so like Sylvie. She stands with her hands straight at her sides, mouth and jaw set like granite. Jonah stands and kicks my leg with his boot. I hear myself groan. *Shut up, shut up, old man,* I say inside, coward that I am. I don't say anything aloud. She's careful with her glasses. She places them next to my tooth on the side table. She tugs at the bottom of the beautiful Irish cabled sweater that she made for me when I wasn't quite so fleshy. Does she have anything on underneath? I don't know. Why don't I remember? She pulls it slowly up to cover her face and I see she has on a purple T-shirt with no writing. When she's removed the sweater, she drops it to the floor. It falls into a heap around her feet.

She stands again, still as a dead tree. Her arms cross her

chest, and her jaw sets hard. When Jessie sets her jaw, she isn't kidding around. She said once that she isn't stubborn. She just makes up her mind and doesn't change it.

"Is that all? You think you're naked, do you? You had a chance." Jonah saunters over toward me as if he were on a Sunday stroll in the park, stops directly in front of my knees, kicks them open, and aims. "One shot is all. No need for any more. It wouldn't kill him right off, of course. Might not kill him at all."

He stands back and takes the pistol in both hands and points it. I close my knees, try to protect myself. I can't help it. Maybe he should get it over with.

"Oh, go ahead, you fucker," I say. "Shoot my goddamn balls off."

"Stop," she says. "Stop it. It isn't important. Here. I'm doing it."

She pulls out the bottom of the purple T-shirt until it frees itself from the waistband of her jeans. I turn away, but from the corner of my vision I see it flutter down to join her sweater. I know she has nothing on under that shirt. Nothing at all. I hear her kick off her sneakers, and catch her bending to pull off her socks. I begin to make some marks on the paper, just light strokes, nothing definable, anything to keep from looking. But then the jeans fall, drop to her bare ankles, and I watch as best I can as she pushes down her underwear to her knees, pushes the rest of the way with one bare foot.

"Now," Jonah says, "draw your lovely wife. Stop your sniveling and draw."

## 13

## JESSIE

JONAH SITS, WATCHES, waits for me to pull off my sweater, but I'm not going to. Fuck him, as the kids would say. Two can play this game. He's getting up. He's confused. He's scared. But he doesn't move toward me. I'm ready to do something. What? I don't know. Perhaps he is weaker than we are. Perhaps if I refuse to take anything off, he'll be frightened and give up.

He kicks Carl hard on his taped leg. And again. Carl groans like a child. I've never heard Carl groan. He doesn't speak. His eyes fill up and he's going to cry. My Carl. Crying because a madman kicks his leg. My Carl. His hands clutch the pencil. He's scared, too. Three scared people. How crazy is that?

It's easy to pull off my sweater and I'm grateful for the time it covers my face. Carl's smell still permeates the wool, even though it's been a year since he's worn it. My braid catches and tugs at my neck. Jonah's ready to kick again. I know he is.

Well, I'm not going to budge. He can kick me if he wants. What else can he do? He can damn well rip the clothes off himself. I'm not stripping.

What's he doing? What? He kicks at Carl, smiles at me, grabs the gun with both hands. He's going to shoot Carl's genitals off. Jesus. He's going to.

"Stop," I say. "Stop it. It isn't important. Here. I'm doing it."

My God. He was going to. I swear this time he's really going to shoot. And what does it matter if I have no clothes on? I undress slowly but steadily. Just like college art class, I say to myself. I've done this before. In front of a whole class. And for money. I can do it here for love. Carl doesn't even open his mouth. He's just going to sit there and draw his naked wife, as if he were a student and I were the paid model. He doesn't look at me. He resembles a dying man, a soft, amorphous mess taped to a chair.

This Jonah is nuts. But he's smart. That's why he's hard to trick. And this isn't really like art class. I don't have a robe to put on between poses. I don't have the choice of walking out. If I stand still, he'll back off. That's it. He'll get confused and then I'll grab the gun. I stand like a step dancer waiting for the music to begin.

What's wrong with me? Am I weak? Stupid? And how can he keep going with those pills in him and no sleep and all this fear? I'm exhausted and I haven't taken any pills.

I've never been modest. My friends in college wondered

how I could strip for money, albeit art-school money and not money from some sleazy joint downtown where girls sucked up coins into themselves. I've heard about those places. No, I'm not modest. But I'm old now. My breasts hang like two deflated sacks and I'm not proud of them.

But I don't even try to cover myself. Why? Jonah stands beside Carl.

"Now," Jonah says, "draw your lovely wife. Stop your sniveling and draw."

Jonah backs away as if to get a better perspective. I close my eyes and pretend I hear students scribbling, voices saying, *I can't seem to get the arm right. How can I fix it? The angle of the hip is too severe.* I hear the sound of the charcoal against the paper. He's drawing. I stand still as a guard at Buckingham Palace. I can't bring myself to pose, to change my position, and no one asks me to.

He sniffs. When I open my eyes, I see he is crying over the sketch pad. *Oh, Carl. I'm sorry.* He draws over the dampness until the paper tears; then he moves to a dry spot. Jonah doesn't even look at the drawing. All I can detect are some dark lines.

"Move," Jonah says. "Look like you're enjoying it. Relax."

"Relax?" I ask. "Put that fucking gun down and I'll relax."

Carl's head jerks up from his work. I think he wonders if his lovely wife would say such a thing. "Jessie?" he says. Nothing else. Just my name uttered in astonishment.

Jonah moves toward Carl as if to kick him again but he stops short when the telephone rings.

"You answer this time," he says. "Say anything even a bit suspicious, I shoot his damn testicles off. Got it?"

"Got it," I say, amazed at my own brazenness in my unclad state. It will be Douglas House again. I'll let them know something is wrong. I've seen that done in movies. They ask a question and I answer something entirely different. When I reach for a towel hanging on the back of a chair, Jonah shakes his head and points the gun at Carl's crotch. The phone rings again.

"Hello?" I say into the receiver.

"Mom? Is this Mommy? Hello? Are you there?"

"Yes," I say.

"Is he there? Did Ralph get there? Isn't he cute? Hello?"

"Yes," I say again.

"I'm in Belfast. I've got my dress. It's lace and off-white and down to my ankles. I charged it to your account at Britts. Mom? Are you all right?"

"I'm fine."

Jonah watches me with the gun pointed at Carl. The corners of his mouth twitch and his tongue licks at the white spit collected there. Ralph. I knew it. Did I know it?

"Well, thank you for calling."

"I'm going to hitch," Sylvie says. "I'll be home by dark. Wait till you see me in the dress. Mom? You sound weird."

"Yes. I am."

Good or bad to have Sylvie here? What if she walks into this scene? I try to speak softly so Jonah won't hear. Why doesn't Carl make some noise? I don't even know what to say. I'm freezing.

"Maybe you should stay the night in Belfast. Just charge the motel to us. I'll pick you up in the morning, dear. Sylvie?"

"Pick me up now. You never loved me. You never thought I could find a man who loved me. Pick me up now. I'll wait at the doughnut shop. That's where I am now. Eating a lemon-filled doughnut."

"It's Sylvie, isn't it?" Jonah grabs the receiver from me. "Hello, my darling." His face softens. The fingers of his left hand release their tight curl around the gun and I will it to drop to the floor. "Their car. It's at the garage. Won't be ready until tomorrow. We'll all come and get you together. We don't want you hitching a ride, do we, Jessie?" He arches his brows at me and expects me to answer. I shake my head. His gaze drops to my nakedness and I try to curl my body, try to conceal myself. "Yes. We're all here together. We're on a first-name basis . . . Yes. We're getting on great. By morning we'll be old friends."

Carl's doubled over, his head leaning on his lap, his face away from us. The pencil rolls across the floor. For a moment I think he's dead, but he adjusts his head, and the toe of one shoe taps on the other. He's given up. Has he given up? What if we both give up? Is that what Jonah wants? For us to give up?

Now Jonah turns away and speaks softly into the phone. "Sylvie, darling. My luscious dolly. Yes, I love you. You know that. Do you love me? Do you?" He slumps into the chair by the telephone. "Oh, God. Thank you. Thank you for loving me. Thank you."

When I reach for the towel again, he lowers the receiver and stands. If Sylvie knew about the gun, would she love him? I remember when I stopped loving Harry, my twin, my best friend in the whole world. After it was all over I loved him again, but it was different. Funny how you can turn love off and on. I was only a kid. Seven or eight. We had our own language that no one else understood. We were inseparable. Our father paid little attention to us and that was fine because we had each other. We were roughhousing at the top of the stairs when I saw him go off balance. I knew he was going. I grabbed for his shirt but it slid right through my fingers. I remember the feel of the cotton slipping past my thumb. What a strange thing to remember. Did I make it up? Did I try hard enough? Could I have held on to that shirt?

I can hear the thudding in my mind any time I choose to conjure it up. Thud, thud, thud. Thirteen steps. And Harry howling at the bottom, blood spurting out of his thigh. Father thought I'd be devastated, but I hated him. I hated him for being hurt. I had no one to talk to. No one to play with. Months in the hospital with the broken thighbone and the infection that developed in his hip. Bone grafts. Body casts. And me, left with dotty old Gram while my father hovered around Harry's hospital bed. I never told them how I felt. I never told anyone. I wasn't allowed into the hospital and it was months before I saw him. Would I have tried harder to save him if I'd known how much attention he would receive? Of course I tried as hard as I could, but I was a child. I no longer think as a child.

I love him now. But what is love, anyway? I think about it sometimes. And what is Sylvie's love for this boy?

"She loves me," Jonah says. "Your daughter loves me."

"Would she love you if she knew how you were treating her parents?"

"I have to do this. I said I'd prepare the way. God told me to know you. *Know you.*"

I tuck the towel around myself and he doesn't speak of it. I'm afraid to put on my clothes, but the towel doesn't seem to rattle him.

"I love to touch her," he says. "Her skin. It's like marble, smooth, firm. She has a scar on her leg, her thigh. Did you know that? I kiss it sometimes. Poor, hurt Sylvie. My mother's dead."

"Oh, I'm sorry."

"I killed her. That's why this has to be done right. I loved her and I killed her."

"Why did you kill her?" I ask. Carl raises his head to listen.

"Don't you remember?"

"No. I'm sorry."

"In the papers. The boy in the well. That was me."

"In the well?"

"Yes. I have the article. In my wallet. I always carry it. To show people. But you don't show your trophies, do you, Carl? You don't show your victims."

"His victims?" I ask. There is no answer from anyone.

The gun is only a foot away from my hand. Jonah is gentle. Thinking about something far away. A beautiful mother who is dead, perhaps. I reach like the itsy-bitsy spider toward the hand holding the handle of the gun, but when I touch it he pulls away. It's all too fast. Everything. The noise shatters the quiet and I feel the rush of air on my foot. A bullet bores into our wood floor inches away from my bare toe.

"My God. What are you doing?" When Carl attempts to stand, the sketchbook slides from his lap to the floor by his feet. He totters and falls back into the chair.

Jonah rips the towel from me and tosses it toward the kitchen. "Enough of this. Back to drawing. Pick up his stuff."

"What?"

"Pick it up. Look, his pencils rolled under the chair. This will be all. I just want to fit in. I want you to love me. You can't love me until I love you. And I can't love you until I know you."

Oh, this is making perfect sense. I just know that he is capable of killing us. I have no doubt of that. Why? I have no idea. But in his mind this all makes perfect sense.

When I bend to pick up the sketch pad, my breasts hang empty and flat. I can feel him watching me. My belly hangs, too. My baby belly, Carl calls it. My eyes close and I wait for a heavy belt to come down on me. Why do I think that? I was never really beaten and certainly never with a belt. I suddenly miss Harry. And my mother. My lips form the word "Mom." Mother? Mummy? What would we have called her? She was always "your mother" or "our mother." She loved me. Don't mothers always love their children?

Did she even get to hold us? Harry was first. Did she die before she got to see me?

Then I remember Dad and the belt. What was that for? Something Harry did, I think. Spilled something? A bottle of molasses. That was it. All over the kitchen floor. And Dad unbuckled his belt and pulled up my skirt and spanked me until Harry fessed up, and then he did it to Harry. Dad cried later, said he was sorry, he'd never do it again. And he never did. Big welts sprang up on my bum. Gram had to put ointment on them. But Dad loved me, too. What does that mean, anyway, love?

The pencil has rolled way underneath the chair but my fingers push it out so that I can pick it up. When I place it on Carl's lap, I stroke the side of his reddened cheek, but I don't feel anything. Where's the love? Where's my love? I don't want to cry in front of them in this state but I've lost my love for him. Why? Where is it? Carl, the light of my life, the man who kisses my neck in the morning, the man who fills the kettle too full. I am alone. Naked and alone. Christ. That sounds like the Bible. Naked and alone in the wilderness.

"Now, pose. Something interesting. I won't shoot you, mother of Sylvie. You're the temple from which she came. But I'll do something bad to Mr. Man here. Mr. Carl. And I don't think he can take much more."

"Pose? How?"

"One hand on your hip. Turn toward him. Yes. Like that. One foot ahead of the other."

I pull my braid over my shoulder to hang down my chest.

I almost laugh at the ludicrousness of the scene. Jonah moves my hand higher on my hip. His hand is hot on my skin and I think of Sylvie. Of him touching her with those fingers. And what did he do to his mother?

Carl draws as if by rote. He looks up at me. Then down to the paper. Makes some lines. Looks up. Jonah paces around us. Glances down at Carl's paper. Looks at my body. At my belly. I don't move. It's all right. I can do this. Just like the art class. I was one of the best, they all said. My poses were creative.

Jonah rips off the top drawing. "Now that's more like it. Do another one. Change your pose." I put my other hand on my hip. "No," he says. "Kneel. Yes. That's it."

I kneel. I wait for a chance to kill him. Carl draws like a robot, like a man who has never loved anyone, never betrayed anyone, never failed. Just draws and draws. Looks up and down. Moves his pencil across the paper. Fills in shadows with the side of the charcoal.

"Sit. No. Cross-legged. Lotus position. That's it."

He rips off another sketch. "They're getting better, Mr. Carl. Yes sirree. No face, though. Work on the face."

I pose. Jonah takes a few more of the white pills from his pocket and swallows them without water. Carl makes one drawing after another as I change position. It's almost dinnertime. I can cook those chicken breasts. Bake them in the oven. And make a salad. I must be nuts, too. How can I think about dinner?

"Now, spread them. I want Carl to draw where Sylvie came from." Carl rips off another sheet and poises, pencil ready. My God. He's ready to draw. "Spread your knees. More. Wider. Good. The temple. A holy place. Now, Carl. Last one."

I struggle to go to another place other than this house with these men. Mom? If I believed in a God, then I might believe that Mom was looking down on me from heaven, protecting me, helping me through this. I can't stay in this place by myself. But if I go to another place, we'll lose. If my mind breaks, it's over. What is over? My life? Our life together? Sylvie?

The Bible. I think about the Bible. Jonah. What happened in that fish's belly? It's important. We have a Bible on the shelf above the art supplies. I move my head enough to be able to see the row of books, search for the large black leather-bound Bible with the old-fashioned silver letters that my father gave us when we married. Jonah. The Old Testament. He was the angry one. The one who defied God. I'm an unbeliever, but I know my stories. My legs are cramping. Jonah stands behind Carl for a better look.

"I'd like to look at the Bible," I say. "Please. It will help me understand you better."

"Understand me? What's to understand? I'm the boy in the well. I'm the boy no mother could love. I'm the end of the line."

"You're Ralph, aren't you?"

## 14

### JESSIE

I KNOW I TOOK a chance. A stupid chance.

"Ralph?" he says.

There's no such person. Ralph? Ralph? Jonah spits as he yells "Ralph" and shoots a hole in the couch, which splits the already fraying cover, and one in my beautiful yellow pine table. I think there are six bullets in a cylinder but I don't mention it because perhaps Jonah has lost track. One in the floor, one in the couch, and then the table. That means there are three left. Then I remember the window. Two left. One for each of us. None left for Sylvie. I think there are more bullets on the shelf. Are there? Carl? Are there?

"I like this shooting," Jonah says. "I like the noise. I like the fluffy white stuffing spread all over that cover. Don't you like the fluff, Carl?"

Carl looks up but says nothing. He has shrunk today.

Like a diminishment of stature. I take this moment, the moment when Jonah is concentrating on Carl, to shift my position, cover myself.

"What about the Bible, Jonah?" I ask. "Do you mind if I read something in it? We could talk about you. About your mother. I'm sure she loved you. All mothers love their children."

"How would you know? And you don't know my mother. She's dead. I want to hear about Carl, here. I think he has a story to tell, don't you, Mr. Man?"

It's as if Carl has vanished. His bulk sags into the chair, ankles still taped to the chair legs, but Dr. Carl, miracle mender of corroded joints, has gone. He avoids my eyes. He looks at nothing. Was it last night that we made love? I can't imagine. It's dead. His sack. His manhood. The part of him that slides into me while he breathes on my mouth. Gone.

"Well, Carl? Tell us a story."

"No," he says. His lips barely move when he whispers the word.

"How about that last drawing. Hold it up for us. That's right. What do you think, Mrs. Model? You like it?"

I'm spread open in black and white, like Eliot's "patient etherised upon a table." There's no detail, just limbs and in the center a great gaping hole. I don't like it. My clothes are nearby and I consider trying to put them back on. I'm cold and the towel is only a small bath towel. It's October and the kitchen window is open. An osprey drops his fish on the beach. The gulls leave their boulder to fight over it. Am I in the same house? The house we live in? It would be easy to slip away to that place where crazy people go. I'm almost there. And there is Harry in a heap at the bottom of the stairs, howling for his long-dead mother. Why do I think of Harry?

"So, Mr. Carl, you're not a Jew. What were you doing in the camp? Your mama really get shot behind you? Running away?"

Carl searches my face. I must have told Sylvie. I must have. I'm not sure Carl even remembers telling me. Such a private thing.

"I'm sorry, Carl," I say. And I am. Truly sorry. "You told me once. Do you remember? I guess I told Sylvie. I'm sorry."

"Sylvie tells me everything," Jonah says. "For instance, I know that your dog just died. You had a miscarriage after the kids were grown up. I know that mister kisses missus every morning on the neck. You did it this morning, Carl, didn't you?"

Carl struggles to keep himself together. I can tell. I know everything about Carl but I've never seen him like this. "Yes," Carl says. I think he's practicing. Trying to come back to the land of the living.

"I know that your beloved Sam fucked his girlfriend in your bed when he was fifteen. Aha! You didn't know that, did you? And your brother, what's his name?"

"Harry," I say. I'm surprised to hear myself answer but it seems a chance to keep away from the world of the crazy, just to answer a simple question.

"He's crippled, isn't he? One leg shorter than the other.

Fell down the stairs when he was a baby. And even the great hip doctor couldn't fix him. I know all about that. You see? I know everything. Almost everything. Except that there's something wrong with Carl's story."

"That's a private story," I say. "Carl lost his family. Leave him alone."

"What about the violin, Carl?"

"What about it?" I say.

"I want Carl to answer. Cat got your tongue, Carl?"

Carl doesn't answer. I've never heard him play that violin. He says it's from another life, that he no longer plays. I once suggested that we hang it on the wall because it's pretty, but Carl didn't like the idea. What about the violin?

"I'm going to take a pee," Jonah says. "I'll leave the door open and I don't want to hear anything except for that infernal car engine."

I'd almost forgotten about things like eating and sleeping and going to the bathroom. When I wave to Carl to get his attention, he turns away. I think about how to cut the tape from his legs, get him on his feet, be ready to tackle Jonah when he comes out, but there's no time. He's back, adjusting his pants.

"Jonah," I say, "tell us what's going to happen tonight, before we all go together to get Sylvie in the morning. What would you like for supper? Chicken breasts? I have a good recipe with tomato and mushrooms."

"Supper? I'm not hungry. You'll be my family, won't you? When Sylvie and I get married. She loves me, you know."

"Yes. I know. Perhaps I should turn off the car. It's going to run out of gas and then we won't be able to get Sylvie."

"Stay right there. I don't really trust you. You tried to hit me with a rock. We have to get to know each other. I want you to like me. You like me, don't you?"

"No. I don't like you. I'm freezing and I have no clothes on. And you're making me sit on a hard floor. How could I like you?"

Jonah, as if he were a kind man, unfolds an old plaid blanket that we keep on top of the dry sink and holds it out to me. I stand and wrap myself in it. He gestures toward the couch. But he still has the gun and it's pointed at Carl's head, so I walk, barefoot, and settle myself on the far end of the shot-up couch, as far away from the exploded fluff as I can. It's not the time. The time to escape. It's coming. I know it is, as long as I can keep myself away from the crazy place.

"Thank you," Carl says from his chair.

Jonah settles into the rocker, his feet planted square in front of him, the gun still gripped in his hand. A waiting game. Is that what this is? I can wait, too.

"We have work to do," Jonah says. "When I know all about you and you know all about me, then we'll be a family."

"I'm not sure that's what—"

"That's right," Carl says.

"And then we can go to get Sylvie."

"Did God tell you all that?" I ask.

"God doesn't talk to everyone," he says. "Only a chosen few. I'm one of them."

"Did he say to hurt us?"

"He said to become intimate with you. How else can I do that? He told me to know you. Because we're going to be family."

"Tell us your story. About the boy in the well."

"No. Not time yet. We need to hear about Dad."

"Dad?"

"Mr. Carl. We don't have much time. That's why I need the gun. Makes things go faster. Moves things along. Do you think you'd tell me everything I need to know if I didn't have the gun? Do you think if I just said 'please,' you'd spill all your secrets? I think not, my man. Are you a man?"

My feet press against my thighs, still ice cold. When my feet get cold at night, I wiggle them against Carl's warm pajamas, but I wonder if he'll ever wear them again. If he dies, who will warm my feet? If we die, who will live in this house? Sam and Charlie will use it summers, bring their families, tell the children, *This is where your grandparents lived until that horrible day.* What happened on that horrible day? What will they be telling the children? And Sylvie. Will the boys look after her?

"Let's hear your story, Carl. If you tell it right, I'll untape your legs. Won't that be nice? And then we'll all have chicken breasts with mushrooms in tomato."

"That's the story," Carl says. "My family was all shot. We were trying to escape."

"Nope, Mr. Carl. I don't think that's the right story. Why the fish? Why the tattoo? Why aren't you circumcised? And the violin."

"They were shot behind me. I kept running. I don't know what happened."

"The violin, Carl. The violin. I know about it."

"What about the violin?" I say.

It's funny, Carl always has the violin nearby, but always in the closet. In our house in Connecticut. Then here during vacations. Then permanently here. But always in the closet. I've touched it. Held it the way you would perch a violin under your chin, just to try it out, always very carefully because it's Carl's. I think it's the only thing he kept from before the war.

"What was your mother's name, Carl? You're not a Jew, are you, Big Man? I know what's written on the violin."

"Carl?" I say. "What's on the violin?"

"There's nothing."

"Oh? That's not what Sylvie says."

Carl's face breaks. Something is on the violin. I remember now. Faded ink on the back, barely readable.

"Please," Carl says. "Please leave us alone. That violin has nothing to do with you."

"Oh, but it does, Carl. Tell us what it says."

"Why don't you go get it?" I say. "It's in the closet."

"No," Carl says. "No. Please leave it alone."

"What does it say, Mr. Big Man?"

"Nationalsozialistische Deutsche Arbeiterpartei. Property of the party."

"The party? Cocktail party? Birthday party? What party, Carl? What party?"

"The Germans." Carl speaks slowly as if he hadn't said those words for many, many years and isn't sure how they sound anymore. "Their party. It was their violin."

"But it is yours, Carl. You're a Nazi, aren't you?"

"No. Never."

"But it's their violin. And you love it. Why didn't you get rid of it if you hate it? But you don't hate it, do you?"

"They took my violin before the camp."

"Time for the truth," Jonah says. "Sylvie told me. And you know who translated it for her? Mr. Hans. She wrote it out for him and he translated it."

"Why have you kept a Nazi violin?" I ask.

"Yeah, big Carl. Why do you keep it nice and safe in your closet?"

The fear of being shot is replaced by a more terrifying one. I am afraid of what I don't know, of not trusting Carl, of not knowing who I am. Sylvie? Hans? Yesterday we worried only about where Sylvie had gone, and now that worry seems impossible. Now we worry about who we are, whether we are a family at all.

"Carl," I say, gently as I can, not because I feel tenderness but because I need to know, to calm my terror. "What is it? What is the truth?"

"Shall we get it? Shall we read 'Property of the Nazis'? What's your name? Göring? Himmler? What's your father's name? Adolf? Your mother. What was her name?"

"Valentina," Carl says.

"No," I say. "It's Chantal."

"No, Jess. It was Valentina."

"Valentina? What kind of a name is that? What about your father?"

"Stefan," he says. "My sister, Nonni. My name, Veshengo. My mother called me Veshi. It means 'man of the forest.'"

"What about Carl? That's not your name?" I look at him,

my husband of forty years, and I can't find him. The man there is old and frail, his flesh doughy, his face haggard. The blue fish on his bare arm covers secrets like Veshi and Nonni. "Jensen. Was that your last name? Is it my name? Jessie Jensen? Am I not Jensen? What about the children?" I search him for the familiar. His pants. His hair. But everything seems askew. "What is my name?"

"Reyes," he says. "It's the first time I've said that name since . . . since nineteen forty . . . I don't know. I don't remember."

"Veshi Reyes," I say. Carl releases a sound from his throat as if it had been there for many years, choking him. His chin trembles. "It's a nice name. Why? Why, Carl?"

"It was a time, Jess, back then, when you could create yourself. No one had papers. It was best."

"See?" Jonah says. "I was right. He's a fucking Nazi. Did you know that, Mrs. Carl?"

Jonah sits as though he is watching a play, and I am embarrassed to be talking in front of him about private things. He looks back and forth, from the blanket-covered nude on the exploded couch to the cadaverous mound taped to his chair. It's funny. Is it? How could it be funny? I suppress the giggle that pounds at my throat to come out. I'm no longer who I thought I was. Am I Jessie Reyes? What kind of a name is that?

"A Jew, Carl?" Jonah asks. "A Pole? A Russian? A German? What's the answer, Carl?"

"No, I'm not a Jew. Why does it matter what I am? I made a good life for my family."

"Your family?" Jonah asks. "Your mother? Your family? Your neighbors? Did you turn them in? You made a good life for them?"

"No. I mean my wife. My children. I'm a doctor. A good doctor. I'm known all over the world. I'm a good doctor." His voice breaks. "What does it matter?"

Does it matter? If Jonah weren't here, I'd rush to Carl, kiss the top of his head, cut the tape on his legs. But I'm almost grateful that I have no choice. I don't know him. Veshi Reyes?

"It matters to me, Carl," Jonah says. "We can't have secrets. Now. Your mother. Did you make a good life for her?"

"I was a child. I was only seventeen, Jess."

"And I was only four," Jonah says. "What did I know? It was dark down there. And wet. And I kept so quiet. No one knew I was down there for hours and hours. I remember it. They say I couldn't remember something from when I was four. But I do."

"My family's dead. That's all."

"Not all. Who killed them? God? Rats? Who, Carl? Did you turn her in?"

"It was a war. Crazy things happened during the war."

"You're making me angry, Carl. And what happens when I get angry? Do you want to find out?"

"I am a Gypsy," Carl says. "A Rom. A Gypsy, my Jess. And I was ashamed. It was easier not to be one. What did it matter? My family was all dead. Everyone."

"A Gypsy?" Jonah says. "I thought you were a German. A Nazi. I thought that was the secret."

"A Rom. A Gitan. A French Gypsy."

"What happened, Carl?" I say. "Tell us what happened."

We sit, silent, waiting for Carl to speak. I want to know, too. I want to know the father of my children. I want to know why his back looks like a chessboard. I want to know how he escaped. I want to know about Valentina and Stefan and Nonni. Was Nonni young? Pretty? Did someone shoot her in the back? And why has he kept a Nazi violin? But I can't ask the questions aloud because I'm afraid Carl will disappear. And Carl's right. What difference does it make? Is he a different man? No. But. Well, yes. He is a different man.

"It doesn't matter," Carl says. "It's another man's story. A man who was just a boy. It's a boy's story."

"Tell me the story," Jonah says. "And when Sylvie comes, we'll tell it again, won't we, Carl? She'd like to hear the story, too."

"Do you promise to let us go?"

"Of course. We'll have dinner. The chicken, remember?"

Carl begins his story, which is for me, not Jonah. For me, because I don't know who I am. I need to hear it.

"This is a relief of sorts," Carl says. "It's been a solitary story for so many years. I'm sorry, Jessie. I wanted to tell you but I thought it would be a burden to you. It seemed easier not to tell."

"Could you cut the tape?" I ask.

"When he's finished."

"We traveled with other Gitans, Gypsy people, in a kind of a family. We were musicians. Violin. And my father sang like an angel. My mother didn't dance, like some of the other women. She played the concertina. My sister, Nonni. She danced. She was only twelve when they came to take us away. They shot our horses. They carved away a section of rump from my father's horse while he yelled its name over and over. Carmen. That was the horse's name. The flies swarmed into the carcass before we left. The buzzing. Loud. Loud."

"That's good, Carl," Jonah says. "But there's more."

"Could you shut the window?" Carl asks.

Jonah almost forgets the gun on the side of the chair when he goes to the window. I could have taken it. I could have. But he knows that. I see it in his eyes. He closes the window without a sound, as if he were a guest and had been asked to do a favor. I thank him and he nods toward me. His mother must have loved him. At least when he was a tiny boy.

"One young German—he couldn't have been more than seventeen—shot Nonni's dog in the face while he watched her reaction. Just for fun. There was no meat on the dog. It was thin and old, almost dead anyway. There were police and soldiers there with the Germans. It was in southern France. The French hated us, too. My cousin jumped on his horse and rode off into the marsh of the Camargue while they raped his mother. She didn't utter a sound, perhaps for fear her only son would come back to try to save her. I don't know whether the bullets reached him or not. I never saw him again. Perhaps he's still alive. His name was Charles.

"They pushed over our caravans and lit them on fire. My uncle wouldn't touch his wife because of the fluids the other men had left in her and because she was naked in front of all of us. We rode in the back of a truck away from the marsh. My sister never cried over her dog. My father sobbed all the way about Carmen. That's all we had to eat for over a week, that raw hunk of meat from Carmen's rump. My father didn't touch it except for pulling off a piece for his old mother. They let us bring a change of clothes and the violins. I played all the way to the camp. Nonni danced. I remember that. She sat on the floor of that filthy truck and danced with her arms and her face while I played the violin. The women sat around her because she had begun her menarche. They circled Nonni and my aunt who was raped, to keep the *marimé,* the unclean, from spreading to the men while they chewed off small pieces of Carmen to feed to the children. We were taken from one camp to another, still in France, I think, although I'm not sure.

"The last journey was to Birkenau, to the Gypsy family camp. That's where they tattooed my arm. Then they took our violins. Doesn't that sound nice? A family camp. The younger children thought there would be games and dancing and kittens to play with. There were thousands of us from all over Europe. But they kept us together in families, just as they said. We had to sleep touching and bathe from the same foul bowl, men and women together, and my uncle Luis couldn't touch his wife because of the *marimé* and went on the fence."

"On the fence?"

"Against the wires. Threw himself on the electric wires. Oh, Jess, this is a horrible story. I didn't want you to hear this story. They left him there, jerking with each pulse of the voltage until he was black and leatherlike. Then they took him off. The night before, he had told her he was sorry, but he couldn't touch her. He loved her but he couldn't touch her ever again."

"Carl," I say. "Carl. This *marimé*. It's about unclean things. When a man touches a woman? Is that it?"

"It's complicated. It sounds foolish. But my people—"

"Your people? They are my people, too. I want to know. Please."

"We can't touch certain parts of other people. We can't wash upper body and lower body in the same basin. There are many things. If you violate them, you are unclean. It is very serious. Very serious. You wouldn't understand."

"I'm Jessie, remember? I'm your wife."

I'm sure Carl won't retell this story and I wish I had a pen and paper. What would Jonah do if I retrieved Carl's sketch pad and charcoal? I seem to be settling into a comfortable corner of the couch while I listen to a story told by a man I don't know. My fingers encircle the end of my braid, pick at the elastic as if to find something familiar. My shoulders are bare but my feet are warming up against my thighs. After this is finished, I'll cook the chicken and find some way to stop him. And then what of Sylvie? If I harm her lover, will she hate me? I can't hurt anyone. But I almost threw the rock. If I had the gun in my hand, could I shoot him? In the arm? In the head? I don't know. I look at Jonah. He's slumped in a chair watching us. He looks young, scared. And he's still holding the gun.

"Terrible things happened at that camp," Carl says.

I search his face for something. Why do I find it astonishing? I knew he was in some kind of camp. Did I think it was like the summer camp where the children went? What in the hell did I think it was?

"We were there for almost two years. We kept track of the seasons and the days. Blistering heat in the summer and razor-sharp frozen mud for months, slicing the soles of our bare feet. I was one of the lucky ones, my father and I. We didn't move rocks back and forth from one pile to the other like some did. They gave us violins to play in the orchestra. One of the others traded instruments with me when I realized that he had received my old one. They had written 'Property of the party' on the back in black ink, but it was mine. Not a Nazi violin. Mine. We played our violins while rows of Jews walked methodically toward the showers. We played marches and military tunes and sometimes lullabies disguised as dances.

"During the day, if I wasn't required to play, they carved up my back, one square at a time, sewed on skins from dogs and cats and horses and hedgehogs and God knows what. They allowed a week for the graft to either take or slough off. I think they grafted the square of skin that they cut off my back onto another man's back. There was no anesthetic and when I called out, they beat the soles of my feet with rods. None of the pieces stayed on longer than a month. They left my private parts alone. But Nonni. They put her under a machine. To kill her eggs. She was only twelve.

"My grandmother. They broke her arm because she hid

a small piece of bread under her hair. She was no longer of any use. My father tried to turn away when they stripped her clothes from her and marched her to the gas, but they forced us to play, turned his head toward her with their truncheons." Carl's voice is soft, as if he is telling a bedtime story.

"Sometimes we wore our clothes. Sometimes we were naked. For a Gypsy, that is very difficult. We tried not to look but the guards knew how hard it was for us and whipped us if we closed our eyes. But we were in a family camp. We stayed together. Some of the couples still had relations in the dark of the night. I heard them whispering to each other, felt the bunk creak."

"How did you get out? Why are you still alive, Mr. Carl? Why you, when all the others died?"

"I was sixteen, and then seventeen. They were going to kill us all. Everyone knew that."

"Well? Why didn't they kill you?"

"Carl. You don't have to continue," I say. How could I have not known this? How could I think he lived in a nice bunkhouse, with soup for lunch and stew for supper, and repaired shoes during the day?

"Sometimes they brought me out to the village of Auschwitz to play for a wedding or a large party. They lent me a pair of shoes and a waistcoat. Not the whole orchestra. Never both Father and me together, although at times he went alone, too. Usually four or five of us, singers, violinists, horn players.

"I got to know the truck driver, Marcel, who was a conscripted young Pole, not even eighteen. I don't know what happened to him. He spoke French. I think his mother was French. He'd lost track of his girlfriend, Inga, I think her name was, until the day she arrived by train at Birkenau with her suitcase and danced all the way to the gas, listening to me playing a gavotte with the orchestra. He was grateful to me for that. She loved to dance. He said she never knew where she was going because of the violins. He rigged up some gear underneath the truck for a person to hang on to, a strap to go around the waist. I think he had done it before. We'd heard rumors that we would be gassed. I was seventeen."

"And what, Carl?" I ask. "What happened?"

"He put my violin in the cab of the truck. No one would question him. He often transported the musicians.

"I crept underneath in the early morning before daylight, and no one saw me. My arms encircled metal bars, and my bare, blistered feet lay along the exhaust pipe. The belt clipped around my waist cut into a skin graft that had become infected. I could smell the pus. I hung under that truck for hours while I waited for it to leave for supplies. It was parked near our barracks all day in the heat of August. Marcel said he had no idea when it would leave, that I had to trust him. I promised to send him money after the war. I sent it to the address he gave me, but it came back. You see? That's how I escaped."

"Why the story?" I ask. "Why the crazy made-up story of running away and your family being shot in the back? Did they follow you? Were they shot?"

"It was two days before the whole camp went to the

ovens. Thousands of people. I've read about it at the library. They took them, orchestra playing, until they took the orchestra. They all died. There were no Gypsies left in Birkenau. And then they moved in more Jews. I think they needed the room. I don't know."

"That the right story? You got it right this time? You got a lot of stories, Mr. Carl."

"I didn't want to leave my family but I was so young. I was small. Not like I am now. Small and thin. Starving. Stinking with infection."

"That long day," I say. "So, the truck left?"

"Yes."

"Yes, Carl? Yes? That's all?" I ask.

"My father was playing in the orchestra by the time they realized that I was missing. But my mother. They brought her out. I wish you could have met my mother. And my sister. Thank God my grandmother had gone already."

Carl speaks between sobs, when he can. He sits with his face in his hands, raising his head only to speak the next words. He is broken. Am I the only one not crying? I cannot imagine tears. It is all too hideous. I tuck my arms underneath the blanket, touch my belly, where my children grew.

"They were naked. Both of them. I could see only their feet and halfway up their legs, but I saw enough to know what happened. I saw too much. They whipped Nonni bent over a stool until she ceased crying out. I couldn't see much but I heard everything. I watched her feet jerk with each stroke from underneath the truck. Why they didn't catch me I'll never know. They shouted at my mother to tell where I was or they would beat Nonni again."

"Did she know, your mother?"

"My mother knew nothing. How could she? She couldn't see me. They sent for my father. I watched his clothes drop to the dusty ground. He helped my mother hold Nonni up so she wouldn't fall, wouldn't be shot. I could see her useless feet and lower legs, bloody from the beating. When I closed my eyes, I saw her in that truck, dancing with her face, her eyes, her arms. They shouted at my father, 'Where is he? Where is he? Where is your useless son?' I almost revealed myself. But I was seventeen. They would have killed us all."

"It wasn't your fault, Carl," I say.

Carl weeps quietly in his chair. He doesn't respond. When he finally looks up at me, I see more than sadness in his face. A kind of horror that I know I will never entirely forget.

"There's more, isn't there? Is that why you stopped?" Jonah seems fueled by the story. He talks faster, paces, his head down. "It's too painful? Carl? Are you awake? Remember the chicken dinner. I promised. When you're finished your story. But you're not finished, are you, Carl?"

"No."

I can barely understand him. "Enough," I say. "No more. He can't stand any more. Isn't that enough?"

"Intimacy through art. Through stories. Intimacy through honesty. Don't you get it, mother of Sylvie? Don't you understand? God said to *know* you. How can I know Carl if he won't tell the truth? There's more. I can tell."

"Please. He's told you everything. How could there be any more?"

"There's more. There's more, isn't there, Carl? Do you want me to whip the little lady? Don't make me do that."

"They held a pistol to my mother's mouth, made her open her mouth, close her lips around the barrel. I couldn't see. But I heard them shout the orders, heard my father groan, heard my sister call out, 'Mama.' My God, why didn't I show myself? Oh, my God. The rest of it, I saw with my own eyes. I saw it all. My sister. Blood dripped down her chin from where she bit herself."

"Well," Jonah says, "I guess that's enough, Carl."

"No. It's not enough. You wanted to hear it. I can't stop now. The others. They tried to turn away. Three were shot. My aunt was one of them. My father loved my mother. He did what he had to do. He thought she would be saved. My sister did it for me. She spread herself on the Nazi dirt and let our father do what he had to do. They made him lie naked on her, his own daughter. The shame. They laughed.

"Before he could stand up, the guard pulled the trigger on the pistol that was in my mother. They left Nonni there in the dirt. Hours later when the truck began to roll out the gates, Nonni still lay on that hard dirt alone. I tried to speak words she could understand on my mouth, but her eyes were vacant and so dark, dark like a raven's eyes. That's the last I saw of her."

"Your father?" Jonah asks.

"They took him away. I don't know what happened to him. Perhaps he lived to go with the others to the gas."

"Tape his arms," Jonah says. "Just while you cook the chicken."

"I'd like to get dressed," I say. "I can't cook with the blanket around me."

"First tape his arms."

# 15

## CARL

I FEEL NAKED although it is Jessie who wears no clothes. This time the tape is tight around my arms. Was it yesterday that Jessie pressed the old skin on the back of my hand? Then I had never hurt her, never used my hands against her. But what now? He has hung the drawings up all around the room with thumbtacks, even the ones of the pine tree. But the drawings of Jessie. God. Where are the saviors? Where are Hans and Marte? Doesn't someone know we are suffering?

My Jess returns to the couch and adjusts the blanket, pulls her bare feet under her. His couch. Where he lay watching the videos. I try to make myself look at her, to reassure her that everything will be all right, that Jonah will go away, that I will dress her gently and make tea and warm biscuits. But I'm ashamed. I make myself look at my hands. They are swelling from the tight tape, from their own culpability.

144 • Cynthia Thayer

The car engine coughs and chokes and then dies. Out of gas. That's no solution for escape now. We all wait for Sylvie. Is she coming? My family is in ruins. What if she comes? What if she doesn't? Perhaps it's almost over, *n'est-ce pas?* Jonah sits quietly at the kitchen table, leafing through our old photo albums, the gun placed in front of him as if it were a water glass. My arms are held firm against the arms of the chair. If I stand I could whack him with it, but he will shoot. The tape crosses the belly of the fish on my arm. I order God to intervene. I haven't believed in God since Poland, but what else can I do?

From his pocket, Jonah takes more pills, swallows them with tea. My pharmacology information on that kind of drug dates back to medical school. It's probably amphetamines. More and more.

"Carl? What ya looking at? I like the album."

"Please. You've done enough. Just go and we won't call the police."

"But Sylvie. What about Sylvie? I've come to prepare everything. I can't leave."

His clothes hang off him as if they were meant for someone larger. He's scared. He doesn't want to do this. His dull eyes drift from Jessie to me as if he's pleading to be comforted, but then his leg begins to jiggle again, banging on the underside of the table.

"I love her. Do you think she's found a motel?"

We don't answer. I think Jessie is too terrified and I have no idea what to say to him. He slams the album shut and tucks the revolver into his pants before he paces again, hugging the album to his chest. When he shoves it into its place next to the others, he hesitates, glances at me, opens the closet. He bends toward the violin, picks it up, turns it over, brings the back close to his eyes.

"I see it," Jonah says. "The 'Nationalsozialistische Deutsche Arbeiterpartei,' the National Socialist German Workers' Party. I studied some German in high school. You could sand the writing off, Carl." He looks at Carl when he makes his suggestion, like a child with a good idea.

What is he going to do with it? He wipes the dried rosin along the frayed bow and tucks the violin under his chin. When he slides the bow across the strings, he tightens the pegs at the neck. I try to connect with Jessie. Now. We could escape. She could escape. She watches Jonah.

Jonah is indeed familiar with the violin. He knows how to tune. The string stretched over the damaged part of the bridge sounds tinny but it is tuned. He plays Chopin. Just snippets of pieces, one into the other. When he plays, his face softens, and his fingers are delicate on the strings. His eyes close while he plays. He changes to Vivaldi. Did his father really take him to violin lessons? I rise, try to pull the heavy chair with me, try to move my feet, but the tape pulls them too close together. He hears me and stops.

"Carl. Here. You play."

"I can't. My arms are taped."

"I'll fix that," he says. "Oh, Sylvie's mother? Please unwrap Carl's arms. And check his legs. Make sure that tape is tight. Can't have him going off willy-nilly."

"What about the chicken?" I say. "You said we would have dinner."

"Shut up about chicken. I'll decide when we'll eat."

Jessie drags the blanket with her, tries to keep it wrapped around herself. Her feet have bunions. I never really noticed that before. When she bends to untape my arms, I stroke her hair with my fingers. She keeps her head close enough to me. She stays at my side, leans her head on my hand. Her face is flushed. Hot. I make a quiet hum in my throat just to let her know. Know what? That I love her? That I'm going to fix everything?

"Where is she? I need her. She's the reason I'm here. Sylvie. My pretty Sylvie. I need to be where she is."

Jonah's hand pats the revolver butt protruding from his waistband. He seems to gather strength from it. Jessie returns to her place on the couch, and Jonah passes me my violin.

I haven't played in years. I haven't held a violin under my chin since I left Europe. The sound of the bow across the strings shrieks into the otherwise-still air. Jessie pulls the blanket up around her neck. It's a good violin. Although I barely remember playing before the camp, I know intellectually that I played with my family in front of royalty and for friends, played dance music and symphonies, folk tunes and our own music, but my fingers seem to remember only regimented Nazi patriot tunes. I play the scale. I play "Happy Birthday," and then it comes slowly, something from the past before the camp. I think it's Hungarian.

"I need to stand up," I say. "I can't play in the chair."

"Play. Tell him to play in the chair," he says to Jessie. "Play something fast. Gypsy music."

My fingers weren't so big then, when I played fast Gypsy

music. They move as if in molasses, playing something from my memory, sad, melancholy.

"I need to go where she is. I need to go where she was."

Jonah paces back and forth while I play. When I stop, he touches the gun stuck in his waistband. I begin again. He takes more of the small white pills from his pocket, swallows them dry. Spittle gathers at the edges of his lips, and the stink of his sweat makes me hesitate. When I close my eyes, I see my uncle, his genitals shot off, naked in the frozen mud of Auschwitz, the smell of fear and excitement mingled, one stink for all of us, guards and prisoners. We all smelled the same. Do I smell my own fear? Jessie's? Jonah's?

"We don't know where she is," Jessie says. Her voice is full, strong. I stop playing to listen. "If you let us call, we can find out."

"She's been here. In this room." Jonah touches the walls, the drawings of Jessie, the side table, the wrought-iron lamp in the corner of the room. "Here," he says, "and here." He touches Jessie's stomach through her blanket. "And here. Play, you son of a bitch. Play or I'll kill her."

He kneels in front of Jessie. I play because I don't know what else to do. I play slowly, pushing my fingers to move up and down the neck, softly so that I can hear what she says over the harsh sound of the strings.

"Sylvie's been here, hasn't she? On you. Inside you. She's sucked at you." He tugs the blanket down, exposing her shoulders. Jessie grabs at the edge to hold it up. He slaps her cheek, not hard, but enough to turn her head and cut into the sound of the music.

"Jess," I say. "My Jess."

Jessie curls up tight into herself. She isn't crying. Her jaw sets hard and I know she can take it, whatever Jonah gives her. She has a new resolve. He jerks the blanket again and it slides down over her breasts onto her lap. She makes no effort to cover herself.

"Let me say this. You two will do exactly what I tell you. Do you understand that? God is with me. It is my mission. Answer me. Do you get it?"

"I hear you," Jessie says.

I nod, murmur something.

"And you. Play. And don't stop. When you stop, I will have to hurt your wife. Do you hear me? I don't want to be doing this. But I have to be obedient. God has mandated. 'Know them,' God said. 'Know.' Do you understand? You. Carl. Answer me."

"Yes," I say.

Jonah pulls the gun out of his pants and holds it to my head while he removes the blanket from Jessie, throws it across the room into the kitchen. She doesn't flinch when he lifts her empty breast to his mouth and covers her nipple with his lips. The urge to turn away is almost more than I can resist, but I watch and play because I must. I can't rise to my feet while I'm playing. I have no balance. And besides, what could I do? Throw the violin at him? That's like trying to kill someone with feathers. Nothing I think of doing to him is possible because of the blasted gun pointing at my head, so I play something my father taught me, for my mother. I see her naked, too, walking barefoot in front of the guard, Hans, who swipes at her bottom with a small whip. "We'll see where he's hiding now, won't we?" he said. "We'll see if little Veshi can watch his own dear mother beaten." And then the crack of the whip hard on her back. It's my punishment. To watch. At that time, all I could see was her feet, her ankles, bare and dirty. My mother, dirty. But I heard everything from underneath that truck. And what I couldn't see with my eyes became vivid in my mind. And as many times as I try to remember her before, in the caravan, dressed in her red dress dotted with mirrors, silver bangles around her wrist, one lone bangle around her ankle, all I see is her bare, dusty feet.

The barrel of the gun rests on Jessie's bare shoulder, the trajectory through her delicate neck, through the thick gray braid that hangs halfway down her back. Even past the notes of the tune, I hear the sucking sounds he makes on her breast. Jessie looks far away, past him through the kitchen window, to the gulls who have come back to the rock and face the lowering sun.

"She did that, didn't she? Didn't she?"

"Yes. Yes, she did."

"I knew it. I feel her with us. Right here." The hand holding the gun relaxes a bit and the muzzle points into the back of the couch until my playing slows almost to a halt; then he moves the gun back to her neck. His hand is gentle on her, cupping her breast in his palm, stroking the skin. "This is what I want. To be close to her. To be where she was. God said, 'Know them. Know her. The mother.'"

He pulls back and grips her ankle, pulls her leg from

underneath her, grips the other. Jessie sits up on the couch. I can see she tries not to show her fear by covering herself. Jonah stands in front of her before he fumbles with his pants, with the button of his jeans. With his other hand he points the gun from me to Jess and back and forth. No. He can't do that. She's not young. She can't take it. Not Jess. When I hear the zipper noise, I stop playing.

"So help me God, I'll kill her if you don't play. Don't you believe me?"

"Carl. Play. Please. I'll cope with this."

"And I want you watching, Carl. W-a-t-c-h-i-n-g. Oh. Wait a minute. You'd like that, wouldn't you, Mr. Carl? You want to watch? Well, we'll see about that."

"Carl. Please," she says. "Don't watch."

"I want you looking at the TV. That's right, Carl. Play. Watch the TV."

"But it's not on."

"Shut up. Watch the screen, stupid. If you look at us, she's . . . Well, you guess."

I begin to play and watch the blank screen of the television, try to drown out the quiet fumbling of clothing.

"I don't want to hurt you, mother of Sylvie, only to go there, where she was, where she grew. Now. On the floor. Keep playing, Carl. Open them. Open your legs."

I imagine I hear her whispering to me, *I love you, I love you, I love you.* Does she love me after all this? I move through the tune, measure by measure, wondering if I will remember the next, but I do. The memory comes from somewhere I can't go, oozes out into my fingers, and I imagine I watch Dorothy skipping down her yellow brick road on the gray screen.

Jonah grunts. He grunts. There is no sound from Jessie, the whispering vanishes, and all the while I play a little tune, a child's tune. For Jessie. For my mother.

# 16

## JESSIE

MOST OF ALL, I'm afraid of the gun going off into my neck. He wouldn't mean to, but it could go off by mistake if he moved too fast or if I turned my head without warning. He's been inside Sylvie, too. I'm sure of that now. I think of my Sylvie underneath him, wonder if she cried out.

I'm alone in this. I don't think Carl can help me. He is only a shell of a man, slumped in the chair, running the frayed bow across the strings of a violin he hasn't played in many years, watching a TV that is not on.

Carl plays a child's tune. I've heard it before. Perhaps he has sung it. Does it have words? Did his mother sing to him when he was a young Gypsy boy? I hum along in my head to distract myself, to keep myself from thinking about what is inside me, to keep myself from that dark, crazy place.

He finishes. Thank God his clothes are on, that his skin doesn't have to touch mine. He grunts, collapses on me, turns his head toward me, closes his eyes. I am afraid to move because the gun is still jammed against my neck. But if he shoots, maybe he'll shoot right through himself, too.

We all breathe together, quick shallow breaths. I feel the metal leave my neck, hear Carl's breath stop. Jonah has moved the gun. It's no longer on me. Carl holds his breath, his lips tight together. I hear a low moan from his throat. Jonah doesn't hear. He doesn't move.

I hear the whoosh before anything else. The violin lands just short of us, slides across the wood floor past us. Carl throws himself toward Jonah, still taped to the heavy wooden chair that was my grandfather's. Jonah scrambles out of me, off me, kneels beside me. Carl heaves himself like a seal toward us, his face red, his mouth open, a wail emitting from his lips. My hand gropes for the base of the floor lamp. Is it too heavy to move from the bottom? Where is the rock? The chunk of granite? I dropped it on the floor. Where is it? Carl's screams become higher and louder. Jonah's hand touches my hip when he clambers to get up. I see the rock. I turn onto my belly and scoot toward it. I'll throw it. It will kill him. My fingers touch the rough edge, and the shot rings out. All at once. My fingers on the granite and the blast of the pistol. What has he shot? Carl? Me? I don't know. The pain I felt has disappeared. I have no pain anywhere. It must be Carl.

"You stupid shit. I told you not to do that. Would you defy the will of God?"

I look at Carl's head first. There is no blood and his eyes are open, focused on me. He isn't dead. Then I see his arm.

Blood covers the blue fish. Was that on purpose? Or just a bad shot? I crawl toward the blanket. Jonah pays no attention to me while I wrap it around my shoulders. Should I try to run? Jonah kicks at Carl's chair and I hear a groan. We're old. We're too old to win.

"You've shot him. Don't you see?"

Jonah seems disturbed by the blood. He bends toward Carl, places the gun on the floor, dabs at Carl's bloody arm with a tissue he's taken from his pocket. If I hit him with the granite, I'd better kill him, and I'm not sure I can. Kill him, I mean. Not sure I can bash him hard enough to kill. I need my clothes on. I wrap my fingers firmly around the rock, pull it toward me. Jonah lifts Carl's arm from the chair, turns it to look at the underside. Carl rants in foreign languages, paying no attention to his bloodied arm.

"Get up," Jonah says. "Can't you get up?"

Carl continues to yell. In French. In German. And in another language. Some I understand. Most I don't.

"You can't get up, can you, Carl?"

"May I help him?" I say.

He retrieves the pistol from the floor, tucks it into his pants. "Come on," he says. "We'll get him up."

I try to avoid touching him when we work to lift Carl and the chair upright, but twice my hand brushes Jonah's. His zipper is still unzipped. Does he know? We rock Carl in the chair, strain against the weight. Carl ceases to yell and helps us by shifting his body.

"He needs a doctor," I say.

"He is a doctor," Jonah says. "Physician, heal thyself."

"It's superficial," Carl says. "It went right past. Grazed the skin."

Carl has not gone to that crazy place, although I thought he might. When we have straightened the chair, I notice that his legs are almost freed from the duct tape, although he keeps them in place. He examines his arm. I can't remember where I left the rock. Then I see it. On the floor by the couch leg, next to our missing set of car keys. Why hadn't I noticed them before? I've searched everywhere for those keys.

"Do you have something?" Jonah says. "For the wound?"

"In the bathroom," I say. "The cabinet."

When he turns toward the bathroom, I creep closer to the rock and the keys. What good are the keys? The car is out of gas. Is there some gas in the garage? Sometimes we keep a can out there just in case. The car. That's it. I could lock myself in and push the horn until someone hears. But what about Carl while I'm in the car?

My clothes are where I dropped them. I don't take the time to put on the underwear. I quickly clean myself with it and toss it into the corner. My T-shirt is inside out but I leave it that way, shove my hands into the sweater arms. I slip the keys into the pocket of my jeans before I pull them on. My legs feel raw as the jeans slip over them. Pain is now everywhere my clothing touches. I hear Jonah rummaging through the medicine cabinet.

"Try some of this," he says when he returns. "Peroxide. And here's a bandage." He doesn't seem to notice that I'm dressed. How could he not notice?

Carl pours the peroxide over his arm. It fizzes at the wound. Would Jonah kill us if he is helping tend to Carl's wound? It doesn't make sense. I don't know. How can I know? Jonah paces, inhales sharply, takes another of the white pills. He stops, presses his hand against his chest.

"Your heart racing, Jonah?" Carl says. "Something wrong with your heart?"

"No. Nothing. Let's have that dinner. Now you know I'll shoot, so watch what you do."

Dinner will give me the opportunity to do something. What? I can't seem to think of anything else except for the rock. I'll make baked potatoes. That will give me some time. I turn the oven on and reach underneath the counter into the potato bag. Is six potatoes too many? I rinse them under the cold water until my hands are numb, and I prick them with a fork before I put them in the oven. The chicken is thawed. I did that yesterday. I'll slice a whole package of mushrooms. I bring the cleaver down over the first batch of mushrooms and realize that Jonah isn't even paying attention to me. I watch the blue veins on the backs of my hands pulse underneath my thin skin. It's hard to remember what my hands looked like when I was young. I'm sure the veins didn't protrude so much. And I think the knuckles were more delicate. They've become coarse, knobby. Is it from cracking my knuckles so much? That's what my father used to say.

I could throw the cleaver at him and cut him somewhere. I hear them talking, Jonah and Carl, and strain to hear what they are talking about. Sylvie's name comes up. Jonah asks

Carl if he's hungry. Just like two men chatting before dinner. Perhaps they'd like wine.

"A glass of wine?" I say.

"Please," Carl says.

Jonah doesn't even look at me when he answers. "If it isn't too much trouble."

I open a bottle of chardonnay with the corkscrew, which I tuck into my other pocket. I touch the keys just to make sure they're still there. The wine splashes into the two glasses that we used just last night with Hans and Marte, and I wonder if they will come down tonight. A wineglass in one hand and the cleaver in the other, I walk the length of our small kitchen, barefoot because I didn't want to take the time to put on my sneakers. I get to the edge of the slate floor and my heart pounds as if it is the only thing inside me. I'm not sure I can do this. Jonah is sitting quietly in the chair next to Carl, waiting for his supper just like a guest in the house or a child home for the weekend.

The last time Sam came for the weekend was almost a year ago. What will he think of all this? Of his father, a Gypsy? His name no longer Jensen. Will the children's names change? If we die, then they will never know. Last February they were all here: Sam, Charlie and Madeline, Sylvie. Snow covered the ground. Charlie and Carl drove into town and rented cross-country skis for all of us and we spent the weekend following one another through the old woods roads along the shore. Charlie and Madeline skied almost on top of each other. Sylvie followed her dad. Sam skied with me. I'm not as athletic as I once was and I'd skied only a couple of times before, but Sam was patient. He teaches first grade, where patience is a necessary trait.

"Come on, Mom," he said. "Just push with one ski and then the other. Glide. Glide. That's it."

"I'm not very good at this."

"It doesn't matter. Are you having fun?"

"Well. Yes. In fact I am."

"Mom? I love my job. I love working with little kids. You taught me that because you love us so much. You love Sylvie, and I don't know how you do it. She's so difficult."

"You always love your children, no matter what they do. You'll know that someday. You will, won't you?"

"Maybe, Mom. Race you back."

We had some hot cider from thermoses we'd lugged all day. Sylvie insisted we rest under the tree with our cider. She skied around and around the tree while we all relaxed with our drinks. She was beautiful that day, purple-and-green-striped socks pulled up over her jeans, a violet sweater that she'd found in a thrift shop, a brilliant red tam pulled down over her ears, thick black hair springing from the base of the hat. She didn't scream. She laughed instead. And Sam and Charlie loved her.

I'm glad Sam has a girlfriend. I hope she loves him as much as I love Carl. And now I'm considering throwing a cleaver when I don't know how to throw a cleaver. What if I strike Carl? What would Sam tell me to do?

Jonah's left leg jiggles and I can feel it through the floor where I stand. Carl cradles his wounded arm. But they both look up at me bringing the wine. I can't do it. I'm not ready.

I slip the cleaver from behind my back onto the counter and replace it with the other glass of wine. Jonah thanks me. Carl nods and accepts the glass.

"Is it terribly sore?" I ask.

"No. It will heal. Jessie? My Jess?"

I turn away. I can't touch him. Why? Perhaps because I love him so much that I'll fall apart. Perhaps because he's weak and defeated. Perhaps because I can't find the old Carl.

The cleaver feels cold in my hand when I grasp its handle to finish slicing the mushrooms. I slice slowly to give myself time to think.

Everything has changed since yesterday. My body and mind are tired and hungry. The car key with its plastic gadget attached to it cuts into my hip. How long before the battery in the car dies? And what about gas? There's a spare container in the garage. Can I get to it? And what about the telephone. The cell phone's in the car. We never take it out. It's just there for emergencies on the road. We've never had an emergency on the road. Once, I called Carl to ask him to pick up a package at the post office. Once, he called me to tell me that Sylvie had called about a new job working in a nursing home reading to old folks. The job didn't last very long but I remember that call and how delighted I was that she was doing something.

My feet pull in the cold from the slate floor. Charlie said to put down linoleum tile because the slate would be too cold and glass would break if it fell. Today is the first time I've noticed the cold. When I lay down the cleaver and gather my sneakers from the living room, Jonah watches me. He is quiet. He touches his chest now and then, wipes the corners of his mouth, jiggles his leg, sips wine, but says nothing when I sit in the kitchen chair and put on my sneakers. When I bend to tie the laces, I smell him and wonder if I can eat a meal with his scent on me.

If I can reach the car, I'll call someone. Charlie's office. Someone is always there. Or 911. They're always shouting in the movies to call 911.

I don't think I can use the cleaver. And I'm not sure about the granite rock. But I'm smart. Does that count for anything? Jonah. Why does he call himself Jonah? Because he's finally doing what God wants him to do. He's been vomited from the belly of the fish and now he's obedient. He knows his Bible. Is he religious? And what of his dead mother? Why is she dead?

I fuss with the salad greens, slice an onion, grate some fresh Parmesan, chop half a red pepper from the bottom drawer of the fridge. Time. Time to think.

The wine bottle is half full or half empty. The men are quiet, waiting for their dinner. I pour more wine into Jonah's glass and he thanks me but touches the gun, which is now in his lap. I don't offer Carl any more. He still has some left. I sit down with them and sip cold water from my wineglass while we wait for the potatoes.

"Do you like chicken?" I ask.

"Sometimes. My mother made roast chicken with lemon."

"How old were you? When she died?"

"Four."

"And you remember the chicken?"

"No. My father made it on my mother's birthday every year. He said I liked it when I was little. He said it's good to remember the dead."

"You were only four? You said you killed her."

"I was four. I told you. In the well."

"Could I see the copy? Of the article? You said you keep it in your wallet."

"Oh, no. I know your tricks. No one sees it. No one."

Carl dabs at his wound with his handkerchief, pours more peroxide onto it. Jonah sips at his wine. I refill his glass.

"What happened in the well?"

"Do you think she found a motel? She should be calling. Where is she? It's your fault. It's your fault she's dead."

"Sylvie dead?" I say.

"My mother. I killed her, you know."

"Oh. How?"

"I fell into the well."

"How did that kill her?"

"Didn't you read about it? Everyone read it in the papers. It was in all the papers."

"I don't remember. Tell me."

"It was at some friend's place. I wandered off. I remember it. Through the woods on an old path. Chipmunks and rabbits everywhere and I wanted to catch one. I walked for a long time. There was an old rusted truck with words on the side and a tree growing right up through the floor. I got in. Pretended to drive it. Vrrrooommmm."

"What happened in the well?"

"There was a circle of stones. Leaves piled up against the wall. I climbed up and sat on the edge. I remember kicking my feet at the inside and little rocks flaking off and dropping into the water.

"I looked down, but it was dark and I couldn't see anything. I was scared. I threw some bigger stones and listened to them hit bottom. Some plunked in water. Plunk. Some hit other stones. There's a difference in the sound, you know. Splosh. Ping. I know the difference. Did you ever throw stones into a well?"

"No. I don't think so."

"It was a big hole. Really big. Big enough for me to lie down right across without my feet or head touching. But of course I didn't lie down across it. Do you think I'm that stupid? Do you think I'm crazy? My dad will lock me up if I'm crazy." Jonah scratches his head, runs his fingers through his bangs.

"Do you think you are?"

"Maybe. But I'm not going back to that Douglas place. Sylvie isn't, either. We're going to get married. Are you happy about that?"

"Should I be?"

"I'm a good person. I'm good to Sylvie. It's just that God tells me things. Would you disobey God if he told you to do something important?"

"If I thought it would harm people, yes, I would."

"Well, you're the crazy one, then, aren't you?"

"I don't know," I say. "Perhaps I am."

"I can work. I went to college. My father says I can't even have children because I'm crazy. He says he won't have any grandchildren. No one to continue his line. That's why I love Sylvie. Children. We're going to have a baby. That's why God set this up."

"Sylvie's pregnant?"

"That's not for me to tell you. She loves me. She knows I can work and take care of her. I'll be a good father."

"Jonah, you're dangerous. You have hurt us."

He pulls the gun from his lap. "I know you now. Both of you. It's over."

"What's over?"

"God's command. I've done it. I know you both now."

"Will you give me the gun?"

"No. Not until Sylvie comes."

"But we're out of gas. How can we pick her up?"

"She'll get here. She'll come herself. I know her. She loves me. She's much older than I am, you know."

"Your mother loved you. Did you harm her? What happened?" I'm getting used to having the gun pointed at me. He aims at my stomach.

He tops off his wineglass and places the bottle on the floor. He raises his glass and whispers to me as if we were friends. "When someone loves you, you have to be careful you don't hurt them."

"How did you hurt her?"

"It was September. Don't you think that was smart of a four-year-old to know that?"

"Yes. Very."

"You stupid bitch." He spits when he talks, wipes his mouth with the back of the hand holding the wineglass. Wine spills down the front of his shirt. "It was in the paper. I have copies. I was scared. There was a crow screaming. I saw it up in the tree. It was looking at me. Every time I threw a stone, the crow screamed. Then I threw a stone at the crow." He laughs. "Got it."

When I shift in my chair, the key chain pushes against me. Can he see it? Then I remember. It unlocks the car. We never use it because we never lock the car. But the gizmo locks and unlocks the doors. The lights flash. And the horn sounds. The horn.

"I didn't mean to," Jonah says.

"Mean to what?" I ask.

"Hit the crow. I'm sorry I did that. That was mean." He lowers the gun and drinks more wine. "Do you like my story? Everyone has stories."

"Yes, Jonah," I say.

"I leaned over really far to see where the stones were going. One minute I was sitting on the rim. The next minute I was crumpled on a wet rock. I could see the sky, a circle of deep blue, wisps of clouds passing by. Isn't that poetic? I write poetry, you know. My lip was bleeding. I was only four."

"How did you get out?"

"I yelled for a long time. It sounded funny down there, like my voice couldn't get out and just bounced around and around the stones. The newspapers said it was only an hour that I was down there alone. What the fuck did they know? They weren't down in the well. They weren't sitting in the wet. I have the article, you know. Right here in my wallet. Tells all about it."

"What happened to your mother?"

"I heard her calling, 'Ralphie, Ralphie,' and I didn't answer. I wasn't supposed to be down in that well. I was bad."

I turn on the overhead light with the wall switch. Carl usually does that. The windows are dark. Has it been a whole day?

"She called and called and finally I answered, 'Mommy? Mommy? I'm sorry.' I saw her face at the top of the well. She was angry. 'What are you doing down there? How did you get there?' She yelled and yelled. Do you think she loved me?"

"She was worried," I say. "Mothers do that."

"She said, 'Come up here this instant.'"

"Jess," Carl says.

"Wait, Carl," I say. "Then what happened?"

"She was beautiful. Hair like Sylvie. Dark. Thick. She leaned over the stone wall, stretching her fingers out for me. But she kept yelling, 'Grab my hand.' I can hear her in my head. I couldn't reach. I tried. I stretched as far as I could." Jonah's glass hangs from his hand, dribbles onto the floor. "Mom?"

"She fell right at my feet. Plop. I was only four. Her head twisted at an odd angle. I kissed her when she asked me to. She couldn't get up. I kept telling her to stand up, get us out of the well. That's a mother's job, isn't it? Well, isn't it? Answer me."

"Yes, Jonah. But mothers can't always fix everything."

"It got dark. I heard dogs barking. 'Yell, Ralphie, tell them where we are.'"

"My mother sang 'Twinkle, Twinkle, Little Star.' I could hardly hear her. Her body didn't move at all. In the morning there was no sun. It began to rain. I remember the rain and the songs. The rain made it look like my mother had great tears dripping down her face, but she never cried. She didn't yell anymore. Can you imagine that? Not once. No more yelling. Can you imagine that, Big Guy?"

"Carl," I say, "answer Jonah. He asked you a question."

"Oh, yes. She loved you," Carl says.

Jonah notices his empty glass and pours more wine into it. He weeps calmly but still holds the gun. I need to keep him drinking and talking.

"She asked me to kiss her all the time. I did. The last thing she said was, 'One more little kiss for Mommy.' I remember that. 'One more little kiss.' The next morning her mouth was wide open and her eyes stared up at the sun and she was hard. Her skin was hard. And she didn't ask for kisses. She loved me, didn't she? Could I kiss you? Just like I kissed my mother?"

All I see is the toddler in the cold well with a dead mother. He has kind eyes. How could he shoot someone? "Yes," I say.

Carl makes a noise of protest but I signal him into silence. I know what I'm doing. Jonah touches his dry lips to my cheek, brushes them toward my forehead, and is gone, back to his position in the chair. "I love you, my mommy," he says, not to me but to his own mother, who is dead.

"Who found you?"

"It was three days. That's what the paper said. I have a copy of it in my wallet, you know. I remember how cold and stiff she became. I tried to close her mouth but her jaw wouldn't move. The rain stopped. I was hungry and pooped my pants. I wasn't supposed to do that. It was very bad. Did you ever do that?"

"Yes. I suppose I did."

"I stepped on her head to try to get out. I grabbed onto the stones, trying to pull myself up. My fingers scraped and I bled all over myself. The newspaper said I was very strong and brave. My father didn't think so."

"It wasn't your fault. You were just a child."

"I heard barking again. I love dogs, don't you?"

"Yes. We had a dog."

"There were three dogs. Blueticks. Funny. I remember that. Wasn't I smart? A man said, 'Are you Ralph?' and I didn't know who I was. A whole group of people looking for me. The newspaper said I didn't speak. They had to get big ropes to pull her up. I didn't see my father for a long time. Until way after the funeral. He finally came to get me at my grandmother's and couldn't even look at me. I don't remember that. He is still alive. He still hates me. He says I killed her. Did I?"

"Of course you didn't kill her. You know that. It wasn't your fault."

"Yes. It was. You know it was."

"Did you really fall into a well?"

"Is the chicken ready?"

"I'm going to fix it," I say.

# 17

# JESSIE

JONAH GULPS THE LAST of the wine while I move toward the kitchen counter to work on the chicken. I hear the slurp, hear him place the empty wineglass on the floor beside the empty bottle, hear the slight moan he makes, hear him stretch his legs out in front of him. The window overlooking the sea is black now. The gulls are quiet and the night creatures haven't begun their nocturnal chatter. The refrigerator motor ceases its drony hum. I hear the breath of both men, one deeper than the other, one faster than the other. I don't know which is which. Once, I hear Carl clear his throat. Jonah picks up the empty wine bottle and places it back down on the floor.

The quiet makes it hard for me to contemplate, as if he will hear my thoughts in the hushed house. The refrigerator begins again when I open it to get the chicken breasts. There are only two. The crinkle of the plastic wrapping rattles my thoughts. Do I have any thoughts? My feet are freezing. I wish I had on some wool socks. That's a thought, isn't it?

The boy—I don't even know what to call him now—is weakening. It's the wine and the exhaustion and the pills. I check to make sure I don't have another bottle of wine, but the shelf is empty. What about cognac? I swing open the cupboard door where odd things like cognac and kirsch and peppermint schnapps are kept. A quarter of a bottle. Enough, perhaps. I don't ask before I pour a half glass into a dusty brandy snifter and bring it out to him. He smiles up at me when I pass him the cognac, but his hand is still on the gun.

How will the night be? I have no more videos. He's seen them all. Will he let us go upstairs to bed? Then I will crawl out the window and drop down to the rosebushes underneath. There's no moon or stars out there. I usually pull the linen curtains shut on dark evenings but it seems silly tonight, so I leave them open. Carl always lights a small fire in the woodstove to take the chill off, but he's taped to a chair. I chop some shallots to fry up with the mushrooms.

How long have the potatoes been in the oven? I've lost track of time. Hours, I think. But no. Not long enough for them to bake. Should I start the mushrooms? I open the oven. I can't remember if I poked them with a fork before they went in. I always poke potatoes before I bake them. I stab a fork into the potatoes, one by one. They're done. The last potato explodes onto my hand; clumps of hot potato spatter my arm, burst onto the floor of the oven.

"What was that?" Jonah says.

I barely hear him over the running water. My hand reddens beneath the cold. My mother smeared burns with butter. Did all mothers do that?

"Nothing," I say. "A potato burst."

"I'd like some more of that brandy," he says.

"Good," I say.

Good. My hand drips water onto his jeans while I pour the rest of the cognac into his glass. He thanks me. How ironic. He thanks me for the liquor.

Carl hears it first. He glances toward the back door. I listen hard until I hear footsteps crunching dry leaves on the stones of the driveway. Halfway back to the kitchen I stop to think. Carl rustles in his chair. Jonah sips the rest of the cognac. The footsteps kick at a stone. Feet wipe on the landing. It isn't Sylvie. She never knows what her feet are doing.

"Hello, you folks. No light out here."

Hans. He clicks on the driveway light from the back porch before he knocks on the glass panel and turns the knob of the door.

"Run," Carl says. "Get help."

"Left the car in the turnaround," Hans says.

"Don't open the door. Run."

"What?" Hans says. "What's going on?"

The door opens a crack. Jonah struggles to his feet. I think he's a bit drunk.

"Go." I've never heard Carl shout so loud. "Go. Get help."

"Sylvie?" Jonah asks.

When I turn my back to him and run to the door, I am ready for a bullet in my back. I yell to Hans to run and slam the door shut. Jonah doesn't shoot me. He shoves me away from the door before he rushes out, revolver waving. I slam the door again behind Jonah, crouch, move toward the telephone. Just as I lift the receiver, I hear the first shot. There is a dial tone. What's the number? Who am I calling? The police. Another shot peals into the night. Hans? The gun. I think it's empty. Nine one one. The bullets on the shelf? Should I hide them? What first? I push the 9 and the 1 and the 1, wait for the ring. Ring. Damn it, ring. He bursts into the house with the gun, jerks the telephone cord from the wall. Where's the rock? Now I could hit him with the rock.

I'm on the floor before I even feel the gun smack against my cheekbone. Carl yells out, "Jesus. Stop it." I look up to see Jonah reloading, slipping bullets from the small cardboard box into the empty cylinder. Six of them again. How stupid. Why didn't I go for the bullets?

"Chicken ready?" Jonah asks.

"The chicken?" It hurts to talk. Maybe he's going to shoot me right here lying on the floor. I close my eyes, listen to his movement around the room. He opens and shuts the oven. He lifts the empty cognac bottle and places it back on the counter. He touches my leg with his foot, pushes at it until I remove my hand from my swollen cheek. Is he checking to see if I'm still alive?

"Your face. Is it sore?"

"Yes." I cry. I can't help it. I weep for myself mostly. But for Carl and his mother and his sister. For Hans. And for

Sylvie. My Sylvie. Behind my closed eyes I see her dancing at the base of her tree. I wrap my arms around her. *Mommy? Yes, my little wood sprite? Can I have a fairy dress? One with sparkles and diamonds and fairy dust? Yes, my darling. Can it be purple and pink and black? Black? Black for the darkness. The fairy darkness, where fairies go in the night.*

Is that the crazy place where Sylvie goes? The fairy darkness? In my own darkness I see them, waves and waves of dancing fairies in purple and pink dresses, in violet waistcoats, waving ribbons in the air. I wend my way through raspberry bushes toward the sparkles, toward incandescent air, toward high voices singing in harmony with one another. Sylvie skips at the edge of the group, waves, calls, *Mommy, Mommy.* Away from Carl, away from a crazy man with a gun, away from burst potatoes and Hans in the driveway. It would be easy. To just go to that place. But then I see him. Jonah. Ralph. Slicing air with a golden sword, prancing the perimeter, his waistcoat shimmering. He's there, too, in the fairy darkness.

My fingers feel the dampness on my sore cheek. I think it's bleeding. Blood and tears. There's no cut. I touch my face all over. My eyes. My mouth. My cheeks. The skin is loose. When did I become old? The swelling puffs over my cheekbone. There, in that spot, my skin is smooth, young, tight. Is he still looking at me? I hear Carl shifting in his chair. He's given up. How does it feel to give up? I'm almost there. I'm almost ready to give up. Perhaps that's what Jonah is waiting for. How will he know when it happens?

I get to my feet quietly. Perhaps he won't notice. He sits

back in his chair, sips at the rim of his empty glass. He smiles at me. His teeth are straight. Did he wear braces? Did his father resent the money? I almost smile back. Years of smiling when someone smiles at me. It's a reflex. But I don't. I just stand looking at the two of them.

"Dinner?" Jonah asks.

"What about the man in the driveway? May I go and check on him? Did you shoot him?"

"Why would I shoot a man in the driveway?"

"I heard shots. Did he fall down?"

"Carl told him to run away. That was bad. That was a bad thing to do, Carl."

"I'm sorry," Carl says. He has given up.

"I'm hungry," Jonah says.

"If you let me check on the man first, I'll make your dinner."

"You'll run away."

"No. Carl is still here. I wouldn't do that."

Would I do that? I could hide in the woods, away from the garage light. Get the gas can, pour gas into the empty tank in the car. No. I don't think I would run away. Jonah would shoot him. I think he would. Yes.

"We'll both go. Then you'll cook? Carl is hungry, too. Aren't you, Big Boy?"

"Yes," Carl says. His voice is small, thin. He couldn't be hungry. Is he going to sit there and eat his potato and chicken?

"Lie down," Jonah says.

"Me?"

"Who else do you think I'm talking to?"

"Lie down?"

"I'm going to tape Mr. Man's arms myself. We aren't going out the door with him almost free, now are we? Down. On the floor. Facedown. You move and I'll blow off Mr. Carl's nose."

I lie down as he asks. Now isn't the time to do something. I hear the tape rip from the roll. It's going to be tight this time. Getting up is painful. Everything hurts. My face. My arms. My battered private places. Inside. Way inside me hurts.

Jonah is ready to go out. "Carl? Are you there?" I say. "Carl?" He looks at me with blank eyes. Yes. I think he is hungry. "Carl."

I say nothing else, hope it is enough to wake him up. Hope it's enough to get him to do something. He'll be alone in the house. Surely there's something he could do, even taped to a chair. On the way out the door, I pocket a small flashlight that we always keep on the shelf by the door.

Jonah makes me walk ahead of him. He leaves the back door open, although the night air is cold. The gun points at my back. I can feel it. Not the gun itself. Its path. The one the bullet will take if he pulls the trigger. Such a simple action. Pulling back a small metal lever. Just a quarter of an inch. Perhaps if it hits my spine, there will be no pain.

"Sshhh," Jonah says. "Do you hear that?"

"What?"

"Something. I don't know what. Just keep walking."

The scene is like a movie. I picture us from about twenty feet away and it reminds me of a bad thriller, a man with a gun jammed into a woman's ribs, she stumbling along, tripping on an untied sneaker lace in the near dark. The light from the garage doesn't expose a body in the driveway. I catch a flash of some night creature, a skunk maybe, although there is no scent. Our footsteps crunch on the loose stones along the edge.

I hear something now. A moan. Should I speak? Did he see me take the flashlight? I don't know whether we should find him or not.

"Jonah?"

"Keep going."

"What are we going to do if we find him?"

"That's for me to decide."

It isn't a question to be answered. My fingers wrap around the small flashlight in my pocket. It clicks on the key ring. Does he hear? No.

"Can hardly see," he says.

"We'll have to get him to a hospital," I say.

"Now how are we going to do that? Be quiet and keep walking."

Hans cries out from the side of the driveway in the darkness. There are no words. Just a cry, a noise of pain. There is no point in walking away from it. Jonah has heard it, too. I pull the flashlight from my pocket and flick it on. The beam is low. I aim it toward the sound but see nothing.

"Give me that," he says.

The gun touches my backbone, pushes me forward. He waves the light back and forth in the drive, searching for Hans, thinking God knows what.

Then I see the silly hiking boot bought in Germany for climbing the Alps. Hans says they help his traction when he walks from his house to ours along the mildly hilly shore route. The boot moves. I see the other.

"Hans? Are you hurt?" I'm not sure what to expect for an answer. Of course he's hurt. Otherwise he wouldn't be lying at the side of the driveway in the dark. Jonah shines the light on him, moves the beam from head to foot. Hans is alive. He stares into the beam.

"Don't shoot me again," he says. He raises his head from the dried leaves. "Please."

"Where are you shot?" Jonah asks.

"I think it's my hip," Hans says.

"Are you bleeding?" I ask.

The beam of light shows red down the thigh of his beige pants. If it were an artery, he'd be dead by now, or at least unconscious. He doesn't answer my question about the blood, just drops his head back onto the leaves and sighs.

"He's not bleeding to death," Jonah says. "Go back to the house. Walk slowly. I'll follow. If you do anything funny, I'll shoot. I have new bullets, you know. Six bullets. That's two for each."

I bend over Hans and whisper to him. Just a few words. I tell him to rest and save his energy. His mouth moves. I think he says, "Don't leave me." On the way back down to the house, I don't look around, just walk in baby steps along the side of the driveway. When I get in the stream of light from the garage, I search for a killing rock, small enough to throw, big enough to do damage. Behind me I hear low voices, rustling, wait for the shot. That's why, isn't it? That's why he sent me ahead. He's going to shoot Hans. Put him out of his misery. I stop walking. The quiet allows me to hear the men better. Jonah's voice is low. I can't make out the words. It sounds like prayer. I place my hands over my ears. I can't listen. Hans is crying, weeping. I hum a song to myself, a lullaby.

# 18

## CARL

SHE WANTS ME to do something. What? What can I do attached to this goddamn chair? Hans is dead. I know he's dead. Probably shot in the heart. Shot in the mouth? Where does a bullet go when it begins at the lips?

Her lips were full. And soft. In the camp she held her lips to my cheek, and I, almost seventeen with a mother's mouth on my face. She said everything would be fine, that we'd get back our horses and the government would buy us new wagons when the war was finished. She said that I was her own little boy, although I was almost as big as she. She lifted my hand and brought it to her lips, kissed my ragged fingers, said that we'd have milk, too, when it was over. Milk and beer and meat soup. Before the war, Mama wore bright red lipstick. That day, her lips were pale, cracked, peppered with sores. What did the Nazis do with all the lipstick tubes?

Jess and Jonah have been gone too long. They should have checked on Hans by now, found him dead, and returned. Where are they? I was supposed to come up with a plan, but what's the point? I can't do anything. I try to lift the chair and shuffle toward the door, but the chair's too heavy. I bend my head down to pick with my teeth at the duct tape wrapped around my arms, and pain shoots from my wound. The tape is tight. But my legs are loose. Why can't I wiggle my foot out? What if I took my shoes off? Then I could slip my feet through easier. I continue to pull my feet from my shoes, try to ignore the pain from the gunshot. A trickle of blood drips down my arm and pools in the middle of the blue fish. My mouth aches where my tooth was. I only had a few teeth left at the end of the war. Most fell out in the camp from malnutrition or beatings. With the shoes finally off, I move my feet back and forth, struggle to pull them from their wrappings.

There are no weapons in the house except for the gun that Jonah has. Are the knives in the kitchen sharp enough? I was supposed to sharpen them, but did I? I think we're going to die here, together. I hope to go first. That's selfish, *n'est-ce pas?* No. I hope she goes first and he makes me watch her eyes glass over and her hand twitch. I deserve it.

Night air blows through the open door. It's cold in the house. There's no fire in the woodstove. I always light a fire this time of year to take the chill off.

I have to pee again. I shouldn't have had the wine. My feet won't come free of the damn tape. I struggle again to pull my feet through, but the socks catch on the sticky tape. I can't do it. I can't even fucking untape my feet from the chair legs. I need my mother's kisses on my cheek, her whispers: *Veshi, Veshi, we'll have chocolate and figs and even marzipan when we get out of here.* And then I imagine her mouth around the cold gray metal barrel of an SS revolver. I see her shivering barefoot in the frosted ruts, watching my father lie naked on our beloved Nonni. Did she know the gun would explode in her mouth? Did she know I was under the truck? Oh, Jesus, did she? She did. Yes. She did.

I'm Mr. Fixit. I fix anything. Hips. Knees. Toilets. Fallen trees. What can I do here? If I could get my feet free from the tape, I could tackle him on the way in. I will drag the chair behind me to the kitchen, get a knife to cut the tape. I'm bigger than he is. Even at my age, I think I'm stronger. He's a boy. Young. Small. But I'm wounded.

Jessie was my first real love after the camp. Camba and I were to be married when we came of age. But that was before Birkenau. She was shot because she stole a potato. Therese, a Sinti Gypsy from Lithuania, begged me to make love to her just before I escaped. I bribed my bunkmates with a piece of moldy sausage to squeeze into some other bunk just for one night and Therese and I slept with our arms around each other. Our bodies covered with thin, parchmentlike skin pressed close. She was afraid the bone rubbing on bone would cause lesions in our skin and we would be selected. When I lay on her, went inside, her hips poked sharp against my belly. She was dry. Like sandpaper. I was dry, too. We were starving. But we loved each other all night. She went to the gas with the others. She must have. I never saw her again.

In college I had a few lovers but no one I really loved until Jessie. After that day in the library when she dropped her books, I saw her walking along the river on a Sunday morning and stopped to chat. I asked her to movies. "Not until I defend my thesis." To dinner, to the coffeehouse. "Not until my thesis is accepted."

One day I got a call. She'd just come home after finishing her orals and wanted to take me to dinner. We went to a Chinese restaurant in Boston, then strolled through alleys and gardens and cemeteries back toward Cambridge. She asked me about my studies, about why I wanted to fix broken joints and where I was going to do my residency. I asked her why she wanted to teach. She said she had a talent for it. We walked through an old cemetery where the lights of the city dimmed and bushes sprang out at us from all directions. Beside the large tomb of some famous old man, she pulled me down by her on the grass and kissed me.

"You're a good man, Carl," she said. She straddled my chest, bent to kiss my mouth, her braid brushing the side of my face. We heard someone walking close by. She held her finger against my lips, stifled a laugh, began to unbutton my shirt. She had no underpants on at all. When my shirt was unbuttoned, she opened it, pressed her dampness against my chest. "You're so good," she said, over and over. What did I say to her? Did I say she was good?

She slid down toward my thighs, unsnapped my chinos, tucked her hand down inside my boxers. I think I unbuttoned her blouse. It was purple. Crinkly cotton, something light. I expected an underthing, but it was just Jessie, her bare skin against the thin fabric. I opened the blouse, like a birthday present, and she leaned forward so that her breast lowered into my mouth. She smelled of nettles and spring earth and soy sauce.

She lowered my zipper so slowly that I felt my whole life go by like a movie. She kept stopping to press her face against the hollow at my rib, breathe in the scent from inside my clothes. When she had pulled the zipper as far as it would go, she squatted over me and tugged my clothes down to my knees. I knew what she was going to do. No one had ever done that before, but I knew. I said silent words to some great, powerful being to let me hold back, keep me from spilling too soon.

"Jessie, my Jess," I said. "*Je t'adore.*" What a silly thing to say. But she didn't think it silly.

When she ran her tongue up and encircled me with her lips, took me in her mouth, I couldn't stand it. I couldn't have her do that. God, I wanted it. But I couldn't. Not in her mouth. She understood. She lay with her blouse open on my bare skin until we fell asleep. When I awoke, I rolled her underneath me and entered her quietly.

She tried to do that again, with her mouth on me, but I said, "No, I'd rather go into you, my Jess." I "went down on her," that's what they called it back then, when we were young, when we first got married, before the children. But I never let her take me in her mouth. No, I couldn't do that.

Jessie's lips are thin, not like my mother's. Her mouth opens wide when she speaks, but her lips are reedy, firm. She's an outdoors woman. Her skin is tanned from her walks along the ocean and sessions painting her beloved gulls standing one-legged on the rock. She swims in the ocean in April and October when no one else in the whole county would dare to. She rows all the way out to the seal rock and back on a good tide. She knits socks. I don't realize that I'm crying until the tears drip from my face onto my arm and mingle with the peroxide.

I hear them talking outside. They're walking back toward the door. Is it too late to act? I glance around for something lethal within my grasp. A candlestick on the side table. Brass. Tall, with sharp edges. I reach for it with my teeth. I bend and touch the bottom of the thing, tip it over and off the back of the table. It rolls away, clatters toward the wall. Do they hear it? It's too light to do damage, anyway. What am I thinking? That I could bash him with a candlestick clenched in my teeth?

Jessie staggers into the house as if someone pushes her from behind. She looks at me. I mean *looks*. Looks to see if I have solved the problem. I lower my gaze, stare at my shoeless feet. I tried. I just couldn't do it.

Jonah shuts the door behind him. I'm glad because of the draft. He's cold, too. He's lost his jacket, and the T-shirt he wears is threadbare. Did he have a jacket? Why can't I remember? I think it was a wool stripe. Looked like a new one. Didn't quite fit him. I always remember whether someone is wearing a jacket or glasses or has short hair or long. I search the room for his jacket. This morning it was on the couch. It's not there now. I think he left it outside.

I can't tell from their faces whether Hans is alive or dead. No one speaks. I think my Jess is disgusted, because she turns away toward the kitchen and fusses with dishes and food. I want to ask about Hans but am afraid to hear the answer. Why don't they say?

"We're going to have a lovely little dinner, Mr. Carl."

"That's nice," I say. I hate myself. Hans is dead because I hated him. Didn't I know that Jonah would shoot him when he ran? Didn't I? Why didn't I just say, *Come in, Hans, please join us?* Then we'd all be sitting down to a chicken dinner.

"Your friend is just fine. He's resting in the driveway. Why'd you tell him to run, Carl? Why'd you do that?"

"He's fine? Isn't he shot?"

"You hated him, didn't you?"

"No. I—"

"He has a small wound. He'll be fine until tomorrow."

"Is Sylvie pregnant?"

"Pregnant? With child? What a question, Carl."

"She's my daughter. I deserve to know."

"You know what you deserve, don't you? You don't want to think about that, do you, Carl? About hell and eternal damnation. We all killed our mothers, didn't we? I'm doing something about that. I'm listening to God's voice. What are you doing?"

"She can't take care of a baby."

"I need to have children," Jonah says. He pops another pill, lays his palm over his heart, gulps a large breath. "I told you."

"But Sylvie can't be the one."

"Sylvie is the one. She is my chosen one. My father says that I'm too crazy to be a father. Well, that's not true, is it? I am a father. I need to be. My mother. She didn't have any other children. Did I tell you she was pregnant when she fell in the well? I didn't know at the time. I heard my father tell someone just last year. He said, 'That kid destroyed my life. Not just my wife but my son. It was another boy, you know. He destroyed the whole line.' I am 'that kid.'"

"I'm sorry," I say.

"But it isn't destroyed, now, is it? We'll be married. In a church. Sylvie wants to be married in a church."

"With her parents present? With her father to give her away?"

"Of course, Carl. We'll all be there." Jonah slumps into the chair, checks his brandy snifter for cognac, returns it to the floor. "Maybe."

Jessie clatters around the kitchen. I hear her setting plates on the table, running water into a pitcher, frying mushrooms in the skillet, adding the chicken, pouring the tomato over it. I hear everything. How can she be cooking with Hans lying out on the driveway and me taped to a chair? How can she cook food for a man who has forced himself on her?

I hear the cupboard being opened. I hear the bottle being set on the counter. Then she walks toward us with an almost-full bottle of peppermint schnapps. I think Hans and Marte gave it to us for Christmas years ago before we retired, before this house. Greasy dust shrouds the bottle, but Jessie doesn't care. Some women would care. They'd wipe it off first. That's what I love about Jessie. She doesn't care about that sort of thing.

"How about a bit of schnapps?" she says, holding the bottle close to Jonah. He raises the revolver enough to show her that he's got it ready, and nods his head yes. She picks up his snifter from the floor and pours until the liquor almost overflows. "Here you go, a little predinner drink."

"What about Mr. Man?"

"No, thank you," I say, because I don't think Jessie wants me to have any, and I hate peppermint schnapps.

I stare down at my socks. For the first time, I notice that they are different colors. Dark green and dark blue. I want to paint with Jess by the tree. Yes. That's it. I want to be there now. Shifting from green to blue, blue to green. Which is this place? The blue? The green? I decide. The tree is the green. This place with blood and fear is the blue. I look at the blue sock, sweep around the room, focus on the green. I can do this. Concentrate. Concentrate on going from the blue to the green. It's where the pine tree is. It's where I can feel Jessie's shoulder blades when I place my palm on her back, when I slide my hand up underneath her blouse. The tree. The tree.

"What the fuck are you doing, Mr. Man? Are you crazy? Something wrong with your feet?"

Drool dribbles onto my pants. I watch dark dots multiply on the material. I am crazy. Yes, perhaps I am. A glass drops on the slate floor in the kitchen. Jessie swears. Jonah jumps up from the chair, knocks over his schnapps. And I sit taped to a chair, unable to keep my own saliva from dropping onto my thigh.

# 19

## JESSIE

I'LL GET HIM DRUNK. In the liquor cupboard there is an almost-empty bottle of tequila with a dead worm sloshing around in it, an unopened bottle of amaretto brought by some dinner guest, and the bottle of peppermint schnapps that Hans and Marte gave us for Christmas aeons ago.

"How about a bit of schnapps?" I say. I don't know how anyone can drink the stuff. If he doesn't like it, I'll open the amaretto. "Here you go, a little predinner drink."

He sips without comment, gives a small nod. He grips the gun while he drinks. I'm surprised he doesn't make a face, just drinks it as if it were wine or cognac instead of liquor-laced toothpaste. Carl hates peppermint schnapps.

They talk while I finish preparing dinner. I strain to hear but the refrigerator drowns them out. Is there something wrong with the motor? Why is it so loud?

"When you finish your drink, we'll have dinner," I say from the kitchen.

There is silence now from the other room. In my mind, which still seems to be working, I command the telephone to ring, then remember that the cord is detached from the wall. I could have grabbed the cell from the car. Well, maybe not. I could have tried. I make work in the kitchen. Move salt and pepper shakers from the table to the counter and back to the table. Fold and refold the cloth napkins. If there is time for him to have another drink, well, then, good.

"What the fuck are you doing, Mr. Man?" Jonah screams into the still evening. "Are you crazy? Something wrong with your feet?"

What is it? What has happened? Carl seems dazed, gaping from one foot to the other. What's he doing? Am I losing him? A water glass slips from my fingers onto the hard slate and shatters in all directions. Now Carl doesn't seem to be doing anything at all. "Shit," I say, just because that's what I say when glass breaks. Charlie told me that would happen. I bend and scoop the broken shards carefully into my hand and drop them into the wastebasket.

I'm going to cry. I squeeze my eyes shut, command the feeling to vanish. No time. No time. Then I see Charlie opening the door, maybe tomorrow or the next day, or next week, opening the door to our house. What does he see? Carl and me on the floor, bullet holes in our heads? Will we be touching? Do they find semen in the autopsy? Does the house smell? Sylvie could find us tomorrow morning. I panic because I can't see tomorrow. It's out there in a haze, surrounded by shadows. Christ almighty.

Jonah calms down. Carl no longer stares at his feet as if

he doesn't know what they are. While they talk about nothing, I glance out to see if Jonah needs a refill. He holds out his glass, empty, as if he were a dinner guest. I pour. I fill his glass to the very top. The air is saturated with the smell of peppermint. The wild urge to do a soft-shoe up and down the hardwood floor singing "On the Good Ship Lollipop" pushes at me until my feet actually shuffle and tap in diminutive steps. When I try to remember the words to "Tomorrow" instead, only "candy shop" words come to me. *Yoo-hoo, Jessie.* I call to myself in my head and barely hear an answer. But the answer is there. *Yes. I'm here.*

"There you go, Jonah," I say. "Good stuff, eh?"

"Never had this before. It's different."

He's agitated, pacing again with the drink in one hand and the gun in the other. Once in a while he holds his breath, touches his chest, wipes the spit from the corners of his mouth. He's cold, too. I can see that. He's lost his jacket. When did he take it off? If I offer him one of Carl's sweaters, maybe he'll calm down. They say warmth makes you mellow, sluggish. I look around the room to see if there's a sweater draped across the back of a chair or thrown in a corner. Carl's hunter's-orange sweatshirt hangs on a hook by the front door.

"Let me get you something to warm you," I say.

"Warm me? I'm warm."

"It's a chilly night. And the door was open. Have you lost your jacket?"

"No. No. I haven't."

The sweatshirt smells of the woods and of Carl. We always wear orange during hunting season. It's the law if you're in the woods. It keeps the hunters from mistaking us for deer and shooting us. A few years ago a woman wearing white mittens was hanging diapers on a clothesline in her yard with twins sleeping inside the house. She was shot because the hunter thought the mittens were a deer's flagging tail. I think he was fined. Perhaps I should be wearing the orange sweatshirt.

"What're you laughing about?" Jonah says.

I hadn't noticed my own laughter but there it is, coming out of my mouth. "Nothing," I say. "Put this on. It's Carl's. He won't mind, will you, Carl?"

"First you get back over there. I'm not falling for any of your tricks. Back up."

When I'm in the kitchen he places the gun down on his chair and his drink on the table, yanks the sweatshirt over his head, shoves his arms in. I don't have enough time to do anything. He's fast. The shirt is huge on him but he rolls the sleeves up, all the while watching me and not moving away from the gun. I've got to get him away from the gun.

He doesn't argue when I top off his glass. He's had a lot of liquor. Wine, cognac, and now the schnapps.

"The tape."

"What's that, Carl?"

"Cut it. The tape."

"Sure, Carl. When we're ready. Hold your water, so to speak. Speaking of water, do you need the pee pitcher again, Carl?"

"No. Not now."

"Tomorrow." The song won't leave my thoughts. Such a stupid song. It's from *Annie*, I think. That silly little girl singing "Tomorrow" into the face of Daddy What's-his-name. Tomorrow. Sylvie waddles into the house. We are both dead, spread higgledy-piggledy about on the floor. Or Carl is still in his chair, slumped over his knees. She's very pregnant. Jonah tells her, *I found them like this, how terrible, such a nice couple. I just went out for a few minutes. They needed milk. Isn't it horrible? Oh, honey, let me hold you.* Sylvie falls into his waiting arms, sobs, says, *I love you,* to the murderer of her own parents. What does Sylvie do without us? And the baby? What about the baby? Is there one? No, she can't find us like that.

"The dinner," Jonah says. "Where's the fucking dinner?"

He's feeling the booze. His words slur, his head bobs back and forth, he swallows a mouthful of the schnapps, but he hangs on to that gun. The chicken and mushrooms have been simmering in tomato sauce for ages. I sprinkle some dried mixed herbs onto the top, add some fresh rosemary from my windowsill plant. When I sniff the mixture, vertigo makes me lean against the counter. It's the same vertigo that gives me the urge to jump when I'm in the pine tree. I'm hungry. That's all.

"Dinner is ready," I say in as natural a hostesslike way as possible. "You can untape Carl's arms and legs now. He needs to come to the table to eat."

"Oh no, you don't. You little cock tease. Carl can eat in his lovely chair. He likes his chair. You and I will eat in the kitchen."

"What about Hans? He's hungry."

"Hans?"

"The man in the driveway."

"Oh, Hans. The little German man. There isn't enough for him." He wobbles toward me with his drink and his gun. "Is this my mother's recipe?"

"No. It's mine. I don't have your mother's recipe."

"Don't you know my mother? You look like her." He reaches out and touches the tip of my braid, strokes the end. I talk to myself. Things like *Don't fall over. Don't push his hand away. Don't agitate him. Don't throw up.* His breath reeks of peppermint. He's too close to me. *Back up,* I say to my wobbly brain. *Back up.* Does Sylvie talk to herself about Jonah? About us? Does she tell herself to hug me so I'll think she's fine?

I command him to sit down and he obeys. Carl does not remind Jonah about promises he made to untape his legs. Rather, Carl calmly waits for his supper, like a nursing home patient strapped to a wheelchair. Jonah places the gun on the table to the right of his knife and waits to be served like a guest of honor at a reception, except that he is fairly drunk.

"Is she dead? Is my mother dead now?"

"I don't know. You tell me."

"I think that perhaps she is. Yes. I think she is." His words are garbled. His glass still has about an inch of liquor but I'm afraid to pour more in, to call attention to it.

"Did you know she was pregnant?"

"Who?"

"My mommy. Do you think I could have saved the baby? Just cut it out when she died? But I didn't have a knife. No knife for me. I was too little."

"Here you go," I say. His plate is overflowing with most of the potatoes and one of the chicken breasts and a slice of rye bread. If he eats everything he might sober up. I shouldn't have given him so much. I pick up a fork to take one potato back, but he grabs the gun and points it at my face. He thinks I was going to stab him with the fork. Could I do that?

"Stop that," he says. "Just calm down. Keep your distance."

"Are you afraid of me, Jonah?"

"No. I'm not afraid of anyone. Only God. I'm afraid of God."

"I'm bringing Carl his dinner. I'll move slowly. I know, no funny stuff. I know."

Carl sits, ready to eat. I slide a tray with his plate and a glass of water onto the small table next to his chair. I smell his blood. Streaks of it crisscross his arm, smear on his pants, still ooze from the wounds on his forearm. When I pour the peroxide onto his wound, it fizzes as if the wound were fresh, but it has been hours.

"Carl, I'm going to feed you your dinner," I say.

"What are you doing over there?" Jonah says.

"I'm feeding Carl. Unless you want to cut him free."

Jonah doesn't answer and I think he's started his dinner, because I hear the clink of a fork against a plate. When I lift a bit of potato onto the fork, Carl opens his mouth like a small boy, oblivious to his own silent weeping, the tears dripping onto his lap.

"Oh, Carl," I say. "Oh, Carl."

"Jess, my Jess."

"At least we know our names, don't we, my darling."

His lips close over the fork. He chews the potato as I move the fork back to the plate for more. He shakes his head at the second forkful.

"No. I can't eat any more," he says. "My teeth."

"Please be alert, Carl. I'm trying to get us out of this."

"Jess? I'm sorry about the . . . I . . . the shame. It is his," Carl says. "The shame is his. And mine, too. I should have stopped him."

We speak in hushed voices. Back in the kitchen, Jonah eats his meal. I hear him knock something over. The pepper mill? Then I hear him pour the last of the peppermint schnapps, which I left on the table in front of him, into his glass. I try to pick at the tape on Carl's arms but can't even find the ends.

I bend my head to Carl and he kisses the back of my neck, just like he does every day. But today he holds his lips there and I hold my neck for him to reach. His breath warms me.

"It's not your fault," I say. "It doesn't matter. The sex. It doesn't matter. He doesn't know what he is doing." I bring my head back up, cup my palm to his face.

"Is she pregnant? Sylvie?"

"I don't know," I say. "Wouldn't someone have told us?"

"Maybe not. She's of age. And they might not even know."

"What about tomorrow, Carl? What will happen tomorrow?"

"Come over here," Jonah says. "He's had enough."

Because I need my strength and because I have a pain in my stomach, I place a small piece of chicken and remnants of the burst potato onto a plate and sit at the opposite end of the table from Jonah. He rests his left hand over the gun handle, eats with the other hand. His plate is now empty except for one of the potatoes, which he cuts into with his knife. I have a knife, too. Not very sharp.

"When you're finished with your dinner, you can have some ice cream," I say.

Charlie and Sam and Sylvie sat around the small table we had in the old cottage right on this spot, listened to the same words. That afternoon we made ice cream with peaches from our yard in Connecticut that we had packed carefully in a cooler for the long ride up. Carl was at a conference, so it was just the four of us. We bought cream from a farm down the road. Thick and yellow.

They took turns cranking the ice cream machine, although Sylvie insisted on deciding whose turn it was. The machine sat dripping on the counter, packed with ice and salt, packed with the essence of summer. Charlie was only five. They all finished their dinner, even the broccoli, which Charlie hated. I scooped ice cream into their bowls and mine with a wooden spoon until there was barely a smudge left in the bottom of the metal canister, and we ate it without a word, the only sound the clicking of spoons against the sides of glass bowls. Sam was three and a half. Ice cream dripped down his chin and dotted his shorts and shirt. After we finished, I remember kissing all their faces, tasting the flavor of peaches and cream and children and a bit of broccoli. The next day I found chunks of broccoli in the pocket of every child, squished and smeared, in shoes, down socks, rolled in the hems of their shorts. Where was I? Why hadn't I noticed?

People don't do that today. It isn't de rigueur anymore to withhold dessert until plates are cleaned. I don't know what to think about that. If I had small children today, would I let them eat what they wanted? But what about trying new foods? When we have grandchildren, we'll have to decide what to do.

"I'd like some."

"What?"

"I'd like some ice cream. What kind is it?"

"Oh," I say. "Chocolate. Yes. Chocolate."

His head drops and bolts up, as if he is drowsing. A shock of streaked blond bangs flops as he moves. Does he dye his hair? What a strange thing. I remove his plate, push his almost-empty glass of schnapps toward him. He slumps in the chair and his weapon hand drops to his lap. There's enough chocolate for one bowl. When I make the first scoop into the container, he focuses on me, on my hand, on my eyes; then he smiles, nods as if he approves, slumps back down into his chair.

In my pocket, my fingers clutch at the keys to the car, *Wait for the right moment.* Then I scoop another blob of ice cream into the bowl, watch him, watch him succumb to too much alcohol. I leave the empty carton on the counter next to the bowl, place my hand back into my pocket, and wait.

## 20

## CARL

WHY DID JESSIE give him my orange sweatshirt? It's mine. In one pocket there's a chunk of dried bear scat and in the other, a brown pastel crayon and that dangly silver earring that I found by the seagull rock. Private things. Pockets are private. And it's too big for him, even with the cuffs rolled up.

I open my mouth for the fork that Jessie offers me, half expecting her to open hers, too, go *Ah* until I swallow, the way she did with the kids when they were tots. I chew the dry potato just because food is in my mouth, not because I'm hungry. I can't eat any more. My mouth is sore and I feel as if I might not be able to keep the first forkful down in my stomach. A glass of water. That's what I need. But I can't ask her. It's too selfish. I shake my head when she offers another bite. No. I can't eat any more.

She asks me to pay attention. She's got a plan. I'm usually the one with the plans. I'm the plan guy. But I don't have one. Nothing. I try to apologize for her violation but it falls flat. I can't even say the word in my head, let alone aloud. When I kiss her I smell a faint trace of peppermint. We talk about Sylvie, wonder if she is going to have a baby. It's impossible, *n'est-ce pas?*

Jonah calls Jessie back into the kitchen. They sit like a married couple eating their dinner. My mouth is dry from the potato. My lips are cracking. I can taste the blood on my tongue. I should have asked for water.

Underneath the truck the day I left the camp I remember the thirst. The truck was supposed to leave in the morning, but it stayed parked in the yard next to the Gypsy camp for hours. I was only a few inches off the ground, jammed up against the hot, jagged metal and tied in with that leather strap around my back, which cut into my already mangled flesh.

If a guard stooped down to tie his boot, he'd see me and I'd be shot right in the harness. I could see just enough to know what was happening. I saw father's shame when the whip cracked on his body as he tried to get off Nonni. He called Mother's name, touched her dirty foot with his fingertips before they dragged her to the dead cart. Nonni rolled onto her belly to hide herself and lay as if dead, even when the whip touched her legs. They propped my father up, pushed him back into line with the rest. They made them stand there for hours and shot anyone who fell out of line. My last view of the Gypsy camp was of more bodies on the ground than standing. Nonni? I don't know. Father? I think he was one of the bodies on the ground.

When the truck finally drove away from the camp, it was full of SS. Above me, almost touching, was the rusted bottom of the truck bed. A few small holes allowed me to see through into the truck bed, where I'd sat many times with my violin on the way to a party or a wedding at the home of a Nazi Party member.

Through one of the holes I saw a man look directly into my eyes, blink, and look away. His eyes were blue. He was young. Not much older than I was.

The heat was blistering, even for August in Poland. I closed my eyes against the hot metal above me and imagined I was at the Camargue sea, imagined the sand beach and cool Mediterranean water at its edge, the lunch can Grammy filled with fresh bread and berries and chicken and nettle soup in a jar.

My mouth was dry. Worse than today. My tongue traced dust on blood-caked lips like sandpaper on painted metal. The truck jolted with each pothole, and once I almost fell to the ground. I could hear their talk even over the roar of the truck's engine. I can't remember now what they said but I remember them singing bar songs and talking about their girls, the pretty Polish chickies in town.

The hump in the center of the road got higher and higher as the ruts made the previous spring became deeper. Thick tufts of grass swept over my back, and several times, protruding rocks gouged at the skin on my shoulders. I held myself up close to the underside of the bed to avoid being hit. I remember worrying about my violin every time we hit a large bump.

Near town the ruts became more shallow, and the hump lower, but loose stones flew up from the road as the truck picked up speed. Not once did I regret leaving the camp. Not once.

I heard a yell from above me, and the truck geared down until it came to a stop at the side of the road. I pulled myself by my arms up hard against the underside of the truck to keep out of sight, watching boots pile out of the truck. They were having a picnic. A goddamned picnic with baskets full of tinned meat and wine and frosted cake. They would see me if they looked under the truck for any reason. Fifteen of them sat around in the field, passing wine and petits fours. I didn't move the entire time. My dirty body must have blended in with the dark rusted metal because no one noticed me. As the last SS leaped into the truck, my arms gave out and I settled back against the biting leather straps for the rest of the trip.

The truck pulled up to a sidewalk in town and the men climbed out of the back. I hadn't seen a sidewalk in years. I saw high-heeled shoes and dresses slapping pale calves and bottoms of shopping bags. A child peeked under the truck. She saw me. If she had been old enough to talk she would have said, *Mommy, there's a half-naked man underneath the truck.* Dark came and there were no more shoes clicking on the cement. "Wait until the dark," my friend had said. "Wait until there is no one in the street." I hung on to the pipes with my last bit of strength. Where did it come from? Each time I considered dropping down and running into the darkness, I heard footsteps, waited for them to go by, planned again. After an hour of complete silence, I unhooked the leather strap, lowered my feet to the ground, and unwrapped my arms from the pipe. I lay underneath the truck for a while, dreaming about water and cake and a potato.

My violin was there on the front seat of the truck, covered with a newspaper as Marcel had promised. I almost left it there but remembered my mother's words, that my violin would save me. It had saved me before. Perhaps it would save me again. I took the newspaper, too, because I hadn't seen one in years. In the days that followed I almost sold that violin for food over and over again.

I ran through shadows made by a light here and there, pulled a sheet from a clothesline, killed a growling dog with a rock, placed my lips over a rotten apple and sucked the moisture into my dry mouth. I remember how it felt. Like God had spread a banquet before me.

Now, while they eat their chicken and potato, I struggle against the tape around my ankles. Sometimes I carry a Swiss Army knife. I try to feel in my pocket with my elbow, although I know it isn't there. It's beside my bed with a bunch of change and a couple of pens.

"I'd like some," the bastard sitting in my place at the table says. "I'd like some ice cream. What kind is it?"

"Oh," Jessie says. "Chocolate. Yes. Chocolate."

Is Hans alive? It's cool, even for October. He'll be freezing on the chilly ground. In the morning there'll be frost on his clothes, frost on the ground around him. Does he really think I'm a Nazi? How could he? How could he have told

Sylvie? I'm tired. I'm so tired. It's not my fault that he was shot. Or is it? What if I hadn't yelled out and told him to run? I try to think of possibilities but my mind is fuzzy. My eyes close. My chin drops to my chest. Marte. She could come looking for Hans. I won't cry out then.

Why didn't I tell Jessie about the camp and the truck and my family? I answer my own question: I'm a coward. Like when the Red Cross asked me who I was. I had lived for months in the woods, stealing food when I could get it, pulling clothes from lines in the backyards of farmhouses. Once, I helped an old couple slaughter their pig in exchange for some of the meat. They let me stay with them in their attic for several weeks. The woman—I can't even remember her name—brought me warm milk every evening and rubbed salve on my back. She let me touch her hair once because I told her she reminded me of my grammy. I played waltzes for them and they danced in their shabby kitchen in threadbare clothing, held each other close. When the SS came to her door to take food, she explained that I was her grandson visiting to help with the farm.

I had been living on beechnuts from the woods and stolen bread and crows that I killed with a well-aimed stone, when I found out that the Germans had retreated. They asked who I was. Me? I am . . . I am French. That's why I was in the camp. I saw the disgust in the eyes of the woman taking names when a Sinti Gypsy begged her to help him find his family. I heard the words "dirty Gypsy" and decided I could no longer be a Gypsy.

How would they know? They didn't look at our genitals. They never knew that I was uncut, a Gitan, a Gypsy from the Camargue. Perhaps it was better to be French and a Jew.

"Next, please," the woman said.

"Yes. I am next."

"Name?"

"I am a French Jew. I am Carl Jensen. My father, Michel Jensen. My mother was Chantal Comeau. I am a French Jew. My grandparents were Jews. I was educated at the music conservatory."

And I pulled up my sleeve to reveal my number but not far enough to reveal the *Z*. There was no one in my family left to hear those words. All dead. All dead from the guns or the whips or the final gassing of the Gypsy camp. I would never again go to the Camargue. I would never again go to France. The next day I paid a tattoo man to stick me with needles until a fish covered the *Z* and all the numbers. I said I had family in America, and they put me on a boat to New York.

From that day when they asked and I told lies, I denied my family. I thought in French and then in English. Occasionally I'd find myself singing in Gitan, singing my mother's songs. Sometimes in the middle of a hip operation, thoughts of touching a woman not my wife, thoughts of *marimé* and our customs, would come to me, saying, *Unclean, unclean*. The resident would say, "Dr. Jensen, are you all right?" Once, I said, "Finish up," and left the operating room, washing my hands over and over and over.

And my family. The pictures of them in the camp came to me at night when I closed my eyes. That was my punishment, to see them violated, in pain, crying out. It was God's retribution.

But the sound was the worst. *Veshi, Veshi,* my mother's voice, soothing, then the gunshot into her mouth. My violin playing waltzes for the Jews on the way to their death. And the SS barking orders, calling us "*schmutziger Zigeuner,*" filthy Gypsies, scum, dirt. We were dirty. There was no way to keep clean, although I tried to wash every day. *Marimé* was violated constantly. And some of the men who couldn't stand it went to the fence, where their burnt bodies were found in the morning. Would my father have gone to the fence after lying on Nonni if he hadn't dropped to the ground back in the line? I think so. Yes. He would have.

But why did I feel no shame? Why didn't I go to the fence? I didn't slip from the truck, say, *Yes, I am here. Veshi is here. Not escaped. Please don't harm my mother, my sister, my father. Please. I am here.* No, I didn't. I became a French Jew and went to America and became a wealthy doctor who can't fix my own daughter. I can't fix Harry's busted hip. I can't fix this crazy fellow, Ralph or Jonah or whoever he is. I'm so tired, tired, and I can't fix anything at all.

"Carl," Jessie says. She crouches in front of me, touches the top of my head, pushes it back to see my face. "Carl, don't. Things will work out. Don't."

"Sylvie," I say. "I'm worried about Sylvie."

"He's drunk," she says. "He's had a lot of alcohol. Just sit quietly."

"Any more ice cream?" Jonah asks.

"No," Jessie says.

"What ya doing there?"

"Nothing," she says. She leaves me, turns toward him, and walks like an angel, her braid swaying across her narrow back.

"Sit down," he says. "Do you have any more of that peppermint stuff? No. You don't. I know that. Don't you think I know that?"

"I have something else," she says. "I'll open it." It must be the amaretto. She opens the bottle, pours some in his glass.

"My mother. She's dead, isn't she?" He slurs his words. "I think I shot her."

"No," she says. "No, you didn't."

"She's not dead? How wonderful."

"Drink your amaretto. Isn't it good?" she says.

"What's that? Who's that?"

"I don't hear anything," she says.

But I hear something. It's Hans calling from the driveway. The voice comes, faint, through the autumn air, through the closed door. "*Hilfe. Helfen Sie mir. Bitte.*" Help. Help me. Please. I heard those words once after I escaped, uttered by a young SS officer when I kicked his head with my bare feet before I stole his boots. His eyes were pale blue. I killed him with a metal plow blade from the field. The boots were black leather, perfect condition, hardly worn. They were a little big the first time I tried them, until I pulled his heavy wool socks over my own.

I stare at the backs of my hands. What did Jessie see yesterday on my hands? Did she see blood? Or did she see the healing hands of a surgeon? She touched the backs of my hands as if she saw something there she hadn't seen before. My fingers are thick. The other doctors were amazed that I could operate as deftly as I did with such heavy hands. My fingers were smaller then, when I was seventeen. Ripped fingernails, dirt so ground in that the skin turned gray, sores and cracks in dry skin. Perhaps it was truly a different man, someone else, who did those things. Yes. Of course. It was a different man. With different hands. These hands are soft; my wedding ring is too tight now, so that my flesh puffs out around it, and my fingernails are perfectly cut straight across. Yes. With different hands. Someone with a different name. Another man entirely. Yes. That's right.

# 21

## JESSIE

"My mother," Jonah says. "She's dead, isn't she? I think I shot her."

"No," I say. "No, you didn't."

"She's not dead? How wonderful."

When I encourage him to drink the amaretto, he lifts the glass and sips, dribbles some down his chin, slurps from the edge of the glass. I watch the gun constantly from the corner of my eye, waiting for my chance to take it. What will I do with it when I have it in my hand? *Stick 'em up?* Hardly. I've never held a gun before. Carl wanted me to try it just in case I had to use it someday. "Why in God's name would I want to use a gun?" I'd said.

Shooting someone is a bit more indirect than bashing them with a chunk of granite or cutting into them with a sharp cleaver. There's that distance from the gun to the victim that only the bullet connects. It's easier, no? Just pull the trigger, and whoosh, the bullet leaves the gun and goes somewhere else, sometimes into the floor, sometimes into a tree, sometimes into someone's flesh. I could do that. I'm not sure I could hit someone with a weapon held in my hand. A cleaver gripped by its handle? A chunk of rock held fast to my palm by my fingers? No. I don't think so.

Then I see those same hands on Harry's back, hands grasping at his shoulders at the top of the stairs. His shirt was blue with white stripes. I hardly remember anything about that day except for my hands struggling to hold on to his shirt, and then his body in a heap on the floor below. Sometimes I think I pushed him, but then I see my hands pulling him back. And I feel that blue and white shirt sliding through my fingers.

"Drink your amaretto," I say. "Isn't it good?"

"What's that? Who's that?"

"I don't hear anything," I say. But I do hear someone outside the door, calling. German. It's Hans. I can't tell if he is closer than he was, because of the wind and the faint lapping of waves on the shore. The voice is frail. He won't last the night out there in the cold with a bullet hole in his hip. Marte will come looking for him when he doesn't return. But didn't he tell us that Marte was going to Boston to see the children? Why can't I remember? I glance at the telephone. It's still lying on the floor, wire pulled out of the wall. If someone tries to call, will it sound like no one's home, or will it sound busy? If the telephone is busy all evening, will someone find that suspicious and call the police? Will Charlie think something's wrong?

I stick my fork in the bit of chicken left on my plate. It's cold and tough. Overcooked. But I chew and swallow while Jonah sips his amaretto and slumps a little more in his chair. His hand slides away from the revolver but stays on the table. His eyes stare at me. He smiles. Amaretto dribbles down his chin. From his throat comes a humming or a groaning. I can't tell which. His hair flops into his eyes and he turns toward the pitch-dark window. Does he see something out there? It's too dark to recognize anything. The gull boulder is obscured by night.

We're all waiting for something. Carl waits for me to act. Jonah waits for Sylvie. I wait for Jonah to collapse into a heap on the floor, leaving the gun on the table. Waiting is a quiet thing. Like waiting in a doctor's office. Everyone sits and stares ahead or glances through *Woman's Day* or an old *New Yorker*. Once while I was waiting at the dentist's office, an old woman came over and said, "Knitting a stocking? Never see that nowadays." She sat beside me, touched the sock with tentative fingers until the dentist called her in.

I circle my fork on the dirty plate in front of me, picking up bits of exploded potato. They are tasteless, dry, cold. Jonah smiles again, licks at his ice cream spoon. I feel for the car keys in my pocket, trace the perimeter of the key ring gadget. He doesn't seem to notice the clicking sound. I adjust myself in the chair. When the refrigerator hums, I flinch. He sits up, his hand sliding off the table onto his lap. After he drains the glass of amaretto, his hand goes to his chest as if he's waiting for the next heartbeat. The other hand joins it, making him look like a corpse, hands crossed on chest, eyes closed. Can I reach across the table and pick up the gun? It's too far. Why didn't I sit next to him? How stupid.

I think he's forgotten about the gun. Well, let's see about that. With the side of my palm, I push my plate toward the edge of the table little by little so he won't notice. It's a test. How far can I go? When it is almost as far off as it is on, I tip it over the edge. The sound of the plate's breaking on the slate blasts into the night silence. Jonah jumps from his chair.

"What the fuck? What is that? I'm sorry, Daddy. I didn't mean to."

I say nothing. He looks around until he sees the pieces of pottery scattered over the floor. He hasn't touched the gun. He wobbles back to his chair, lowers himself into it, licks the corners of his mouth. His arms hang down at his sides, sway slightly. Yes. I can do it.

"Sylvie will be coming soon, Jonah. Isn't that nice? She'll be driving down the hill any minute. Won't you be glad to see her?"

"Sylvie. Yes. She's beautiful, isn't she? Do you know her?"

"Yes, I know her."

"She's my girlfriend."

"Yes. She's your girlfriend."

We speak soft words at each other about Sylvie in the dim light. His words come slowly, slurred at times. His hands occasionally touch the edge of the table, press on his heart. There is no sound from Carl and the calling from

Hans has ceased. It is only Jonah and I at the kitchen table talking about Sylvie.

The small wall lamp beams its light into the darkness, throwing shadows on his face. How funny, the things you never notice, like which lights you always turn on in the evening and when you do it. We usually eat with candles burning at the table and then Carl flicks on the overhead light after dinner when we read or play Scrabble. Jonah doesn't question Sylvie's driving a car. Doesn't ask where she would get one. He doesn't mention the baby. Oh, Christ, is there a baby? I try to picture Sylvie loving him. I almost can.

Sylvie and I have talked about how she can't take care of a baby. "Someday, my Sylvie, someday when you're better," I lied to her. She'll never be well enough to have a baby. She's almost too old already. If we live through this, Jonah, Ralph—I don't even know his last name—will go to jail or to a hospital with locked doors and bars on the windows. And what of Sylvie? We'll bring her back to Douglas House after the abortion and she'll settle back down to making aprons on her sewing machine and stringing beads on thread. Shit. What am I thinking? If we don't live through this, what will he tell her? What will he say about our last day? What will she think? Who will take care of her? I think I'm near the crazy place. Am I? Please tell me.

Again my fingers find the car keys and the button on the key ring. My thumb circles the button. Should I press it? He's drunk. It's going to work. I press down hard on the button. It works. The horn sounds from the garage.

"Listen, Jonah. Do you hear the horn?"

I press again and again, leave a moment between each press. The horn beeps short blasts each time I press the button, unlocking, locking, unlocking, flicking lights that only Hans can see.

"Do you hear the horn? It's Sylvie. Go and see."

"Oh, Sylvie. Oh, she's here."

"Quickly. Go and greet her."

He smiles at me, a kind but tired smile, the smile of a child at the end of a hard day at play. The gun remains on the pine table, looking like a still-life centerpiece, while Jonah staggers toward the door. I keep pressing the button until he opens the door. I move slowly toward the gun. I have time. I don't want to upset him. The metal chills my palm. Carl begins to speak. I tell him to hush, whisper it across the room. Jonah closes the door behind him and we wait again.

"Jess, hurry. Help me."

"No. I know what I'm doing. I know exactly what I'm doing."

The gun is lighter than I expected. For such a lethal thing, shouldn't it be heavy, almost too heavy to lift? If I put it in my pocket, it might go off and shoot my leg. My pocket isn't big enough, either.

"Jessie, give me the gun."

"Quiet, Carl."

"I'm almost free. Bring the scissors."

"I can handle this."

"Oh, please. Jess. You can't do this alone."

"Shut up, Carl. Just shut up."

Perhaps I won't need the gun. He'll collapse outside and we'll plug the phone back in and call the police. There's no lock on the door. I can't lock him out. My sneakers squeak on the slate floor as I pace back and forth. I raise the gun, point it at the refrigerator. My hand trembles. From fear? From hunger?

In the background, I hear Carl thumping in the chair, calling out to me to set him free.

The living room is warmer than the kitchen area. I sit on the couch near Carl's chair and think. When you push your brain to think fast, it shuts down. Mine is shut down now. I barely remember where I am and why I am holding a gun. He's coming back. The door opens. He's weeping like a child.

"Sylvie's not there. Where is she?"

"Come sit beside me. Come. Right here."

"Mom?"

"Come on, Ralphie. Sit here."

I tuck the gun behind the pillow with the tiny round mirrors sewn all over the front, in a place that I can reach before he can.

"But . . . but I . . . I've forgotten something. You're my friend. What is it I've forgotten?" His legs crumple. He sinks into the couch beside me, his legs sprawled in front of him. His breath oozes almond and peppermint and I notice the zipper of his fly is still down. The opening gapes.

Beside me on the table, on top of some books, lies the remote for the video machine and also the one for the

television. I flick them both on and press play. Sylvie pirou-
ettes across the stage all alone. She was seven. The dance
teacher asked where the natural sense of dance came from.
"Which side of the family has dancers?" "No dancers that
we know of." "But she has such flair and a solid sense of
rhythm that comes from being born with it." "Oh, no. I
dance but just for fun. And Carl? He has three left feet.
Dancers must be way back."

I turn down the television volume. I can't stand the
Muzak. "See? That's Sylvie. Isn't she lovely?"

"My Sylvie. She loves me. She's my girl."

"Yes. She's your girl."

"We're having a . . . we're . . ."

"Hush," I say.

When Carl rustles around in his chair, clears his throat,
I signal "Shut up" with my hand. Sylvie dances around the
pine tree, trailing colored ribbons sewn to her white eyelet
dress and tied to her fingers. Her hair is twisted with flowers, mostly goldenrod. The music turns in her own head,
real sounds that we can't hear. Does the music come from
the crazy place? She leaps and turns, her bare feet pirouet-
ting on the pine needles. When she discovers the camera,
everything changes. Why? Why was it so terrible to film it?
Why did she hate it so? She pulls ribbons off, rips goldenrod from her black hair. I press fast-forward on the remote.

With my other hand I practice my grip on the revolver
from behind the pillow. The handle is warm now. He doesn't
notice because he watches Sylvie covered in white feathers,
dancing her dying swan on the stage in Hartford.

"Jess, don't show that one."

This time she knew we were filming her. The auditorium was full that night, mostly with parents and family of the ballet students. Her swan, sick with pain, suffers alone on the stage until it collapses on the bare wood, shudders, and lies deathlike. The audience sits still for a long moment before they are on their feet, clapping, yelling, "Bravo." And the curtain closes. Each time I watch this, I feel distressed until the curtain calls show her standing up, smiling and bowing, blowing kisses to the audience, her white feathers askew, her hair springing out from the bobby pins we stuck in to keep her bun in place.

"Pretty girl," he says. He doesn't look at me. The television screen holds him rapt. "Isn't she pretty? She's too young to have a baby."

A dancer from the corps brings her a bouquet of red roses interspersed with baby's breath. Sylvie twirls around and around with the flowers, twirls around and around. I'd almost forgotten this part. She twirls and twirls to that music only she hears. She twirls too many times, and when I see the worried ballet teacher hurry onto the stage, I press the fast-forward button again.

She is the loveliest creature in the world. Jonah is right. She is the fairest in the land. She's my daughter and I love her. Do I love only what she used to be? What she promised to be? How about what she's become? All three, I think, although it is difficult when she explodes, spews hatred at us. Her eyes are the worst. When she comes at me shrieking about how much she wants to hurt me, her eyes seem to belong to someone else. But they don't. They belong to Sylvie. And Jonah's eyes belong to him. Does his father love him? Perhaps not. Perhaps it has all been too much for him, the difficult times destroying the attachment of parent and child, the love a father has for his only son. Would he do just about anything to protect his child from some horror or another? Would he?

# 22

## JESSIE

"CAN WE SEE the pretty girl dance again?"

I rewind the video for him, or is it for me? "There," I say. "See her dance? I was there in the audience. That's Sylvie. That's my daughter."

Jonah's eyes close and he rests his head on my chest. Sylvie dances across the stage again, covered in the white feathers of her swan, while I watch. I think Carl watches, too, because when the swan swoons, begins to die, Carl whispers something like, "Oh, God." Jonah pulls his knees up close to him, faces me. I don't want to see his eyes. They open and he turns and watches Sylvie's swan sink to the floor. He nestles against my breast.

"Oh, poor swan," Jonah says. "Poor swan."

"That's your Sylvie, you know."

"Yes. I know. She's mine. Isn't she lovely?"

"She's not ready for a baby," I say.

"The pills. I had some pills."

"Never mind the pills. You don't need them."

"People say we're too sick to have a baby. Are we too sick?"

"I don't know."

"She's going to buy a dress. White. With colored ribbons sewn all over it."

"Lovely."

"Are you my mom?"

"Yes. I'm your mom."

"Do you love me? Remember when you twirled my bangs around your finger? Do you? Mom?"

"Yes. I remember."

"Will you do that?"

I don't answer. I slide my finger across his forehead, under a lock of his hair that hangs there, and twist my finger around and around, allowing the slim strand to slide through. Jonah hums a little tune, very softly to himself. "*Jesus loves me, this I know.*" I join him. "*For the Bible tells me so.*" Where did I learn that? Sunday school? He stumbles, pauses, begins again. He snugs his body closer to mine while I watch Sylvie touch her toe into the cold bay, look back, smile, and plunge into the water. She swims back and forth like a seal. My free hand reaches behind the mirrored pillow. "*Yes, Jesus loves me. Yes, Jesus loves me.*"

Sylvie rises from the cold ocean, her black hair coating her skin like a selkie's. Carl knows. He murmurs, "Jess, please. Please don't." But he isn't a mother. And it's a mother's job, *n'est-ce pas?* It's not the same for fathers.

Sylvie waves to me behind the camera. When I wave back, she stubs her toe on the seagull rock, screams, "Bitch," into the lens. "Bitch. You fucking bitch. I'm never coming here again. Never. You can't force me." I read every word on her lips, remember the sounds in my ears. I continued to run the movie camera. Why did I do that? Why didn't I shut it off, wait for a better moment?

My fingers grip the gun handle, find the important places. I pull back the cock thing as I saw Jonah do, and slide the gun out from behind the pillow. Sylvie and Charlie play badminton across the TV screen. It's the same day as the "Bitch." Sylvie wears white shorts and a chartreuse tank top, her hair now dry and spiraling down her back, swaying with each smack of the racket on the birdie.

Jonah looks at me, smiles, says he likes the girl on the screen, the one playing badminton with bare feet. "Yes," I say. "Isn't she lovely?"

I touch his back with the gun, move the tip up and to the left. He doesn't feel it.

"Jess," Carl says. "Let's call the police. Please."

I don't answer.

Jonah slumps forward and I slide the barrel of the gun up toward his shoulder blades, angle the path down, through his heart and into the cushion of the couch. His bangs are damp and my finger sticks, pulls his hair a tad. I slow down with the twirling. "*Yes, Jesus loves me. Yes, Jesus loves me.*" He sings the song, every word, great pauses between lines. Sylvie picks a spent delphinium and holds it out to Charlie as a present for winning. Can I do this? Can I?

"What ya got there?"

"Nothing. Nothing at all."

"Pretty pillow. Look. It sparkles." He picks at the mirrors on the pillow.

"Yes. Now just lay your head right here."

"*Yes, Jesus loves me.*"

"Watch the boy take the flower."

"*The Bible tells me so.*"

"Jess. My Jess. Don't."

"See the pretty flower, Ralphie," I say.

And then I pull the trigger.

Jonah rises from me as if jerked by heaven with a great hook. When he slumps back down he shudders everywhere. His arm falls open onto my lap. His fingers curl. At the end of his great sigh, his body relaxes on mine, heavy and limp. It is done.

Sylvie slices the air with her racket, begs Charlie for another game. Charlie's too tired and backs off, places his racket on the picnic table, shakes his head. I can't watch Sylvie hit him with her racket, hit him hard in the face. I can't watch Charlie wrest the racket from her and hold her tight while she bites at his shoulder. I press the power button on the remote and the room is still. The scent of almonds charges the air, covers the stink of fresh blood. I feel it, very warm, leaking from his heart onto my thigh. When I search for a hole in his back where the bullet went, my fingers touch the orange sweatshirt, the part covering his heart, find a small hole, like a cigarette burn. There is no blood there. No blood on his back. It comes from his front, dripping damp on my jeans. Sticky and still warm. I think Carl says my name over and over, gives me time in between to answer.

How could he be dead? His bare arm touches mine, flung across me after the shot. His fingers are open now, no longer clenched. Dampness weeps from his mouth onto my clothes. Blood? No. I don't think so. Is it over? No. It isn't over. I lay my head on the back of the couch, close my eyes. Carl won't stop calling me. He calls and calls. He breaks the silence each time. *Stop it. Stop it.*

"Jessie. Please. Answer me."

Do I answer? How? What do I say? The handle fills my palm. There are more bullets in there. I don't know where the first one is. I touch the sweatshirt on his front. Sticky. I slide my fingers up toward his heart. It has exploded. I hesitate at the edge of the crater. Too horrible. Such damage a bullet can cause. I had to do it. I had to.

I think about love. I don't think he felt anything at all. I don't know what to do now. Carl's pleas become louder. He asks me to look at him, to cut the tape around his ankles. But I hum a child's tune, a simple ditty, something about a gray goose, telling someone the goose is dead. It's a nice tune. The words come to me. I sing the words through my own weeping. I think Carl believes that I have lost my mind. Have I? Have I lost my mind?

I can't seem to move. Jonah is heavy against me. I'm not sure I can get up. I lift the gun. It feels heavy now, and cold. Where did the warmth go? Shot in the back. I shouldn't have shot him in the back. I'll have to do something with the gun. I hold my hand at the edge of the couch and release the thing. It falls to the floor. Thud.

"Sylvie, I had to," I say. "Don't you see?"

"Jessie. Push him off and come here. I'll help you."

"Oh, Carl. I . . ."

"Just push. You can do it. Just get out from under him."

"I can't. He's too heavy."

"Jess, Hans is out there. Come here. Now."

Carl never yells. Why does he yell at me now? Hans? Oh. Hans. Yes. He's in the driveway. Oh, God, he's in the driveway. When I push Jonah away from me, the dampness of the blood cools my skin. He's heavy. His hand slides off onto the couch cushion.

I am drenched in his blood. When I stand, I can see stains on the couch and seeping across Jonah's chest, as if the heart continued to push all the blood from his body after it was hit.

"Come on, my darling," Carl says. "Walk over here. Bring the scissors."

I walk across the room toward the scissors. They lift off the hook easily. What did I expect? I don't know. They are sharp. Points. Blades. They're expensive scissors. Stainless steel. Fine honed. Perhaps they're ruined from cutting the duct tape, adhesive covering the blades.

"The scissors," he says. "Bring the scissors."

I pluck the loose end of my braid by the ribbon. "Look, Carl. It's all gray now. Did you know that?"

"Yes, my pet."

I look over at the boy on the couch. He hasn't moved. I

am surprised. But how silly. Of course he hasn't moved. I
killed him. Red covers the hunter's orange on his chest. An
explosion. His heart. Is the day over? I expect to hear police
sirens coming down the drive, but why would they? I de-
tour toward the telephone cord, see that it is intact, plug it
into the jack. When I lift the receiver, a dial tone throbs into
my ear. I lower it back onto its cradle.

"Jessie?"

"I'm coming, Carl."

And Carl. Where has he been? Has he been here all this
time, still taped to the chair?

I place my palm over the blue fish and slide the sharp
points of the scissors between the tape and the chair, close
the blades over the thick wad. I have to cut again and again,
like a child with plastic scissors. The other arm's tape cuts
easier. When I free his hands, Carl reaches up to my face,
very slowly as if the pain is almost too much, touches the
corner of my mouth, runs his finger down my chin, touches
my collarbone.

I bend my head. He holds his mouth at the nape of my
neck and speaks but I don't understand the words. He
speaks softly onto my skin. What does he say? I bend far-
ther, away from his lips, toward his feet. The tape is loose
and the scissor blade slips in easily, cuts through the layers.
I cut slowly. What after this? What do we do after this?

# 23

# CARL

Jessie lowers her hand onto my arm. Her fingers, flecked with his blood, steady my wrist while she slides the scissor blade underneath the tape. She frees my hands. I raise them to her sad lips. She doesn't open them for me, keeps her mouth tight, closed. I feel the corner of her mouth quiver as she lowers her head so that I can touch the back of her neck.

"I love you so, my pet."

"Do you, Carl? Do you really?"

"He would have killed us, *n'est-ce pas?*"

She moves away from me to cut the tape from my ankles, slowly, deliberately, not Jessie's usually quick way.

Blood seeps from the boy, continues to bleed onto his clothes, the couch, pools on the wood floor by the discarded gun. Such things that mothers do to save their children.

The last night in the Gypsy camp, my mother held me while I told her of my planned escape. I leaned my head on her breast and whispered about the brown truck, about Marcel, whose girlfriend danced to the gas to the sounds of my violin, and about how he had rigged up the underneath of the truck so a boy could hide. I pretended she wore her red blouse with the silver threads and bracelets around her wrists and smelled like rosemary and olive oil. She pretended that my hair was clean and that my face was freshly shaven and that I wore shoes on my feet.

"When you see the brown truck just outside the camp, I will be underneath," I whispered to her. "Watch the truck leave the camp. Then you'll know I've escaped."

"You will do it. Run as fast as you can away from this place. Don't eat the green nuts. Wait until they dry. Keep your violin close to you. It will be your salvation. Don't drink creek water. Make nettle soup."

"I will, Mama."

"And Veshi. Don't look back. You'll trip on a root."

"The brown truck, Mama."

"The brown truck. Yes. I'll watch for it." She pulled a chunk of dark bread, spotted here and there with bits of mold but still soft, from her bosom. "Tuck it into your pocket. Don't eat it all tomorrow."

"The man, Marcel. The guard. Don't tell anyone. Not Daddy. No one. He'd be killed."

"I don't know anything," she said. "How do I know where my boy is? Perhaps killed. Perhaps gone into your 'bakery.'" She laughed, then, about the bakery. That's what we called the ovens. I laughed, too. How could I laugh?

And I knew she wouldn't tell. And I knew while I was hanging under that brown truck and she took the revolver in her mouth that she wouldn't tell anyone where I was.

"Carl, I shot him."

"Yes, my pet. You did."

"What will we tell Sylvie?"

"We'll think of something."

"Stand up, my darling. Can you stand up?"

I struggle to my feet, using my hands on the arms of the chair for leverage. My hips ache. My first step is tentative, unsteady. Jessie takes my arm as we walk away from the chair toward the window. When I raise the window, the cold night air surrounds us, chills the room, softens the smells of blood, of urine, of unwashed dishes.

Jessie turns toward me. It is then that I see the streak of blood on her cheek. I moisten my finger and scrub it away, wipe until her skin is red from the rubbing. I have to spit twice to remove it. My arms encircle her. She's small. I sing to her a song from my mother in the Romany language, a song about a little bluebird. The words come from a long-forgotten place, verses and verses. When I finish, Jessie leans still against me.

"Sing again. About the bird."

"How do you . . ."

"What, Carl?"

"Nothing, my pet."

While I sing, her body presses hard against mine as if she wants to become part of me. She opens the collar of my shirt, presses her face against my bare chest. When I finish the song, she continues to hum the tune. I run my hand down her hair, linger at the end of her braid.

"Should we get another dog? A retriever?"

"Oh, Jess. Sure. We can."

"I miss Reba. I miss the wet-dog smell. Remember when she used to run on the mudflats and then jump on the couch? And now. Look what's on the couch. Look, Carl. Look."

"I know, my pet. I see him."

"We'll have to do something."

"Yes."

"And Hans."

Jessie gets her jacket from the hook on the wall, puts it on, zips it, pulls her braid to the outside. She tries the flashlights on the windowsill, one after the other, until she finds a strong beam. But she does not look at the boy on the couch again.

Noises from the shore filter through the open window. Rustlings. Dry leaves. Splashes in water. The night creatures. Jessie's gulls have left the boulder, but they will come back.

I reach for my sweatshirt on the hook by the door before I realize where it is. Jessie opens the back door and steps out into the night, and I follow. Each step is painful. My stiff legs feel weak. Jessie shines the flashlight ahead of us, sweeping the beam around the front of the garage, at the edge of the driveway, underneath the rosebushes. Has she changed? She's still small. But her actions are now slow, deliberate, old. When did that happen? Today? No. I think a long time ago. I have only just noticed.

An owl screeches in the distance. I reach for her hand, but in the dark I miss it, grasp at air. For a moment I panic. Where is she? But of course she is there, just ahead of me, kicking at sticks, looking for Hans.

I see him first, mutter to Jess. She directs the beam toward the dark heap by the edge of the rosebushes. It doesn't move.

"Hans?" Her voice is shrill, loud. Too loud. "Hans."

He's curled up like a sleeping baby. Across his shoulders is Jonah's jacket with the wool stripes, warm, tucked tight at the neck. His head rests on his sleeve. One of his arms is flung to the side as if searching for something to hang on to. It's not his fault, all the killing and the hatred. What if he hadn't run? What if I hadn't called out? Did he think I was a Nazi? And was he? Was his father?

Jessie bends down to him, pulls the jacket away to look. She brushes his hair back, closes his eyes. Why do we close the eyes of the dead? Before she stands, she pulls Jonah's jacket up loosely over his face, straightens his arm. And what of Marte?

I follow Jessie into the house in the near dark. The flashlight beam is almost gone and the light from the garage doesn't shine very far. We don't speak. What is there to say?

This time she holds her hand back for me to take. It's warm. I don't squeeze hard, just hold her fingers loosely until we are through the door.

Jonah's head leans on his own shoulder and he would seem to be asleep if not for the blood. Jessie picks up the blanket she dropped when she dressed and covers him completely with it. Sticking out from underneath the blanket, his feet rest, one on the other, as if he is napping or reading a book.

I glance around the room. Evidence is everywhere yet nowhere. Jessie's underwear is balled up in the corner by the bathroom. Discarded drawings litter the floor around my chair. A ghastly nude of Jessie dangles from a tack beside the clock. A stoneware plate speckled with potato and bits of chicken lies on a place mat at the end of our yellow pine table, a splintered bullet hole as a centerpiece. Jessie's wadded-up tissue balances against her glasses on the side table. My tooth is in there. But the hum of the refrigerator and the sounds of a sudden evening shower pinging on the tin roof are familiar. Is it all right to leave Hans out in the rain?

"What are you doing?" I ask. Jessie tugs at the back of Jonah's pants. The body moves. She is too close to it. Too close.

"His wallet. Here. I have it."

She reaches for her glasses and puts them on, turns away from the body. The brown leather wallet is almost empty. Just a driver's license belonging to Ralph Johnston, and an old photo. It's a woman, young, beautiful, holding the hand of a small child.

"There's no article."

"There was no boy in the well," I say.

"Yes. There must have been," she says.

She pulls out the photo and hands it to me. Behind it, folded and refolded, is a yellowed newspaper article. Before she opens it up, she places the wallet on the side table. One edge of the paper rips. Inside is that same picture, a mother and child holding hands. The article is short. She reads it aloud.

"Local boy and mother survive fall into well. Ralph Johnston, five years old, receives minor lacerations. Marion Johnston sustains compound leg fracture. Both have been released from the hospital and are in good condition despite the ordeal. The two spent nearly twenty-four hours before they were found by a local schoolboy."

"You see? He did fall in the well."

"You were right, my pet."

"His mother. She was lovely. And look. How she adores him. Do you see?" She tucks the article back, places the photo over it, lays the wallet on the arm of the couch. "Carl?"

"I know. Don't look at him."

"Carl, eagles don't mate in the air. Did you know that?"

She moves toward the telephone, raises the receiver to her ear, presses buttons, and waits.

"This is Jessie Jensen. Something has happened. I need the police."

She gives our address but doesn't wait for a response. With the corner of her sweater, she wipes a speck of blood from the back of the receiver before she drops it into the cradle of the telephone. She slumps to the kitchen window, peers out to see if her gulls have returned. It is dark. No moon or stars tonight. She sits in her chair at the end of the table, pushes Jonah's plate over the bullet hole, spreads her book filled with pale green paper in front of her, slides her old hand over the smooth leaves.

There are things to do. I count them on my fingers, just to make sure I don't miss something. We'll have to find Sylvie. And Marte. I'll have to tell them. And the mess. The mess. I walk unsteadily toward the kitchen sink, pour myself a glass of water from the faucet, sit down in the rocking chair. When I close my eyes, I see Sylvie and Jessie dancing, skipping, holding their hands together, back and forth in front of the old pine tree, its branch strong, intact. Jessie's braid is flying behind her, and Sylvie, her Gypsy hair, black as this night, dances like Nonni on the floor of the truck. Dances with everything she has.

"Jessie," I say. "Thank you."

"What's that, Carl?"

"Nothing, my pet. Would you like a glass of water?"

"No. Tea. Some black tea."

"We'll have to—"

"Black tea. Please, Carl. Not now. Some tea."

I fill the kettle and place it on the burner. Water sloshes onto the top of the stove. I mop it up with a sponge before I light the gas. Jessie writes on the paper with black pen and waits for her tea. She looks up from her book and smiles at me. She's scared. I can see it in her face. But she smiles anyway. I lean on the counter and watch the flame of the gas lick the bottom of the kettle.

"I think I'd like to turn the heel. Could you pass me the sock?"

"It's a splendid sock. Do you want the red yarn?"

"For the toe. Yes. For the toe."

I close my eyes briefly and hear my mother singing the song about the bluebird. *Fly, my pretty bird, fly from the cage, fly to the woods and the sea and the mountains. Then, Veshi, run, run like the wind away from this place. Don't lose your violin. Don't turn around. Don't look back.*

After I bring Jessie her tea, after I touch the blue vein on the back of her hand, I look out into the darkness, wonder if there are any gulls back on the rock. The rain drums steadily on the windowsill and I think I will cover Hans with a tarp. On the way out, my foot touches the violin poking out from under a chair. I pick it up and hold it under my chin. One of the pegs is cracked but the body is intact. I bring its neck close to my mouth and run my lips over the tailpiece, place my too-large fingers over the sound holes. She touched these places before she died. My mother's hands held the neck, the fingerboard. It doesn't matter about the writing on the back. And yes, I could sand the paint off. After all, it was stolen from me. The bow lies close to my foot. I bend to the floor and take it in my hand. I pluck one of the strings. Then I place the instrument in the closet and go out the front door to find a tarp.

# 24

## JESSIE

I HAVE AN HOUR or so to write before the others return from their predawn Thanksgiving hike up Schoodic Head. My hands smooth the pale green leaves of my notebook, which stands out strong against the blue of our pine table. When the table was yellow, the book seemed a complementary part of it. Now it appears alien, foreign to the shiny blue, but not everything has to be part of everything else.

The young gulls outside the window fight over some scavenged fish while the others wait for the sun to rise. I cling to my thoughts these days. I write with a new fountain pen filled with black ink that Carl bought me. It was a surprise.

A pair of eagles ascend together from the mist and fly toward our boulder. One settles in the dead spruce near the shore while the other veers off. Why didn't I challenge him about eagles mating in the air? I knew then who he was, didn't I?

I write the date at the top of the page. The teakettle sings on the stove and I pour the steaming water over Earl Grey tea bags. There is just enough to fill the pot. While I wait for the tea to steep, a few large flakes of snow drift past the window. Snow sticks on the boulder, litters the picnic table. It's early for snow, *n'est-ce pas?*

The first word I write is "Sylvie," because that's what I think about these days. I also think about what has changed: We have lost a friend—Hans. We have gained a friend—Marte. We have no dog. We have no liquor in our cabinet.

I write my thoughts about love and life and the human condition. Sometimes I feel as if I know everything there is to know about how and why we behave as we do. Then I wonder if I have a clue why I can't seem to forget that I no longer smoke or that our dog has died or that there is nothing more I can do for my daughter.

I have managed to wash the blood from my fingers. I have thrown away the soiled clothes and the exploded couch. We replaced the kitchen window and filled in the hole in the center of our dining table and painted it blue. We rented a floor sander but now have a depression in the maple floor because we held the sander there too long. We do what we can.

When I turn the page again, the card from Sylvie covers the next page. Not everything is negative. The card is black with primitive white letters: "Barn's burnt down . . . now I can see the moon."

"Sylvie," I write again.

After it was over, after the police found her wandering early the next morning along the road to our house, we walked through the woods to the pine tree, our steps together, our strides identical. I looped my arm through hers and we both wept in our own quiet ways. The broken limb had fallen to the forest floor, spilling Sylvie's hidden village. Scattered around the limb were remnants of her precious family: bits of shell and bark glued together, felt clothing rotted in places, twigs wired to stones, all carefully stored in the crotch of the old pine tree for years.

I knew it would be her undoing. "Mom? My family. You killed my family. You bitch."

When she threw the decaying bits of moss and sticks and bones that had been her "beloved family," I held her as tight as I dared.

"Sylvie, oh, Sylvie, I love you."

"I hate you, Mom. You killed the father of my baby."

"But there never was a baby, my darling."

We found her a new place close by, run by a young family and a good staff. Carl brought her down. She wouldn't get in the car if I was going, too. She says she's never coming home again. I don't believe that. I believe she will come home again and she will throw things at me and curse and that she will lay her face against mine and kiss my eyelids. But for now, I am the destroyer of her family.

There is always a price to pay for every act we perform. The boys say all the right things, but I feel in their embraces and kind words a hesitancy, a fear of having a mother who could do such a thing.

But when Carl wraps his legs around me in the night, I feel he needs me. Last night he whispered, "Jess, I thought I didn't tell you about my life because I thought it would be a burden to you. Now I know that it would be a burden to me, too. It was a selfish thing." And I felt his poor back through his pajamas and wondered how he could have hung on to the underside of that brown truck for so long.

Who am I to think that I will figure it all out by writing in my notebook?

I realize that I have no idea why we act the way we do. I just know that I did what I had to do for my own sanity. I know that it happened so fast that he felt nothing. I write that down but then realize that, like Carl, I am building a case for myself.

I close the book, stare at the back cover, place the cap over the gold nib of my new pen. The place in the center of the table where the bullet went through is smooth. I can't find the wound with my hand even when I close my eyes and trust my fingers. Then I feel the small hole in his back where the bullet entered. It's my burden to feel that hole forever.

The turkey needs basting. I chill the white wine before I begin to peel the potatoes. Through the kitchen window, I see them returning. They stop at the boulder, lean against it as they talk. The wet flakes of snow build up on their shoulders and hair. Marte's hat is covered. I'm grateful she agreed to come for dinner.

Charlie hangs his arm around Madeline, kisses her forehead. Sam's new girlfriend's name is Veronica. Isn't that funny? It reminds me of that old cartoon. She's studying oncology. Carl likes her. They talk about hospitals and illness and surgery. Carl laughs. I can hear him even through the falling snow and the windowpane. I haven't heard him laugh much. Is that Sylvie's moon? The laughter? I wave with my free hand.

Yes, this Thanksgiving will be different. I have a new family, Carl's family, although I will never meet them. They are all dead. Or perhaps they aren't. What about Charles, the cousin who rode into the Camargue marsh?

I have a new husband with weaknesses and sadness and guilt, whom I will learn to love all over again in a different way. Not the Carl who fixes everything, picks me up, fixes my cuts, but a Carl who is real and who needs me now. And his violin. Last week he turned over the corner of a page in the phone book, highlighted "Violins and Cellos Refurbished and Repaired."

And Sylvie. Yes. She's in the dark place now. Her family is destroyed. Her barn is burned down. But she will see the moon. I will help her. We will talk about her father in the camp, and Ralph, and perhaps she will emerge from the fairy darkness dancing.

Carl opens the door. Behind him are my boys with

Madeline and Veronica and Marte. Carl has lost weight in the last few weeks. He walks as if it is difficult to pull his shoes from the floor. But he spreads his arms toward me. Yes. He loves me. I go to him.

"Carl? Why do the gulls face the rising sun?"

"Because they know it's going to be a day full of fish, my pet."

## ABOUT THE AUTHOR

CYNTHIA THAYER is the author of two previous novels, *Strong for Potatoes* and *A Certain Slant of Light,* both Book Sense selections. *A Brief Lunacy* is a Book Sense Notable book. Thayer has led workshops for the Maine Writers and Publishers Alliance and Schoodic Arts for All, and has taught fiction writing at Turnstone Writers' Workshop and the University of Maine at Machias. She is a founding member of the Meetinghouse Theatre Lab and a member of the Wednesday Spinners (of *Wearing Wool* naked-spinners calendar fame.) She lives with her family on Darthia Farm, a waterfront organic farm and mail order business in Gouldsboro, Maine. Visit the author at www.abrieflunacy.com.